KILLER QUEEN

JULIE MULHERN

J & M Press

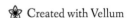 Created with Vellum

For Jennifer,
with gratitude

Acknowledgments

Gretchen, Rachel, Matt - I couldn't do this without you.

Chapter One

Kansas City, Missouri
April 1975

The turquoise AMC Pacer (a fishbowl on wheels destined for the scrap heap) should have been my first warning.

I could have turned my car (a convertible with classic lines sure to stand the test of time) around. I could have made up an errand, met my best friend Libba for a *bon voyage* pitcher of martinis, taken a drive with the top down and the wind in my hair. Anything but what I did.

I parked my TR6, breezed through the front door, and waited for the clatter of claws on hardwood.

Nothing. The dogs, Max and Pansy, were probably in the backyard destroying my annuals.

My packed suitcases—Gucci, a wedding gift from my husband (*for traveling through life together*)—were stacked and ready for a trip back to their homeland. I smiled at the suitcases and the promise they held.

As for my traveling companion, just thinking of him made my heart beat faster.

I never imagined I'd visit Venice with anyone but Henry, but the traveling-through-life-together thing hadn't worked for us. When my painting career took off, he grew bored with monogamy. If he hadn't died, we'd have divorced.

"Aggie?" I called.

My housekeeper appeared in the kitchen door wearing a sky-blue kaftan splashed with burnt-umber daisies. Lines etched her forehead, and her lips drooped into an uncharacteristic frown. Despite the kaftan's bright fabric, she looked ready for a funeral.

"What's wrong?" I set my handbag on the bombé chest in the foyer and peeked into the living room. The empty living room. I returned my gaze to Aggie. "Who's here?"

Her gaze slid away from me. "A visitor. She insisted on waiting. I put her in the study."

"The study?" My late husband's study had resisted all desperately needed attempts at redecoration. Hardly the place for guests. "Is Prudence here?" Prudence Davies was among the host of women with whom Henry dallied.

She didn't like me.

The feeling was mutual.

Prudence deserved to wait in Henry's study. "What does she want?"

The latest addition to my household, a Labrador retriever with obedience issues named Pansy, once belonged to Prudence. Grace, my daughter, and Max, our Weimaraner with an eye toward world domination, lived in fear Prudence would change her mind about giving us the dog and demand Pansy's return.

Aggie did not share their sentiments. "It's not Miss Davies. I don't know this woman."

Interesting. "What's her name?"

Aggie raked her fingers through her hair. Seconds passed. "Aggie?"

"Mrs. Anarchy Jones."

There's a ride at Worlds of Fun, the local amusement park, called the Finnish Fling. Riders stand with their backs pressed against a circle (rather like standing inside a barrel), and the circle spins. Faster and faster. Until the bottom drops out. When I rode the Finnish Fling with Grace, my stomach dropped with the floor and landed somewhere in China (where it bounced like a Super ball). I had that same feeling now. I clutched the bombé chest and attempted to inflate my lungs. "Who?"

Aggie's auburn brows met over her nose. She pressed her hands together as if in prayer and tapped the edge of her fingers against pursed lips. "She said her name was Mrs. Anarchy Jones."

I closed my eyes. Squeezed them tight. If Anarchy had a wife, he wouldn't have asked me to travel to Italy with him. If Anarchy had a wife, he'd have told me. I had to have faith. "It can't be."

Anarchy and I were leaving for the airport in three hours. There was no way—no way—he had a wife.

Was this Mother's last-ditch effort to keep me from traveling to Italy with a man to whom I wasn't married? Would she stoop so low?

Frances Walford was many things—patronizing, high-handed, snobbish—but she wasn't underhanded.

I opened my eyes. "Aggie, I need coffee."

"I pushed Mr. Coffee's button when your guest arrived. The coffee's still fresh."

What would I do without Aggie? Or Mr. Coffee?

"Give me two seconds." Aggie disappeared into the kitchen, leaving me to contemplate my stacked suitcases and the mystery woman in the study. Had she heard us talking? Who was she?

Aggie returned, pressed a mug into my shaky hands, and nodded toward the study's closed door. "She already has coffee, but I'll bring a tray."

"Thank you." I drank deeply, mustered my courage, crossed the foyer, and turned the doorknob.

My late husband's study remained a mishmash of dark wood, plaid upholstery, bookshelves filled with histories, biographies, and dry tomes about war, and a desk the size of Rhode Island. I'd recently packed away his collection of Toby mugs—leering faces were no longer part of the room's ambiance.

A blonde woman had chosen a club chair with a view of the front yard. She'd seen me arrive.

I cleared my throat. "Good afternoon."

She didn't respond.

"Good afternoon." Louder this time. I tightened my hold on the coffee mug and ventured into the study.

Dread, as heavy as the packed suitcases in the foyer, settled in my stomach. I circled the chair.

Mrs. Anarchy Jones slumped bonelessly. Her head hung at a funny angle. And my second "good afternoon" had been loud enough to wake the dead.

Also, she'd spilled her purse. A handkerchief, lipstick, compact, and billfold littered the floor.

Mrs. Anarchy Jones wore a Diane Von Furstenberg wrap dress. Her hair was an expensive shade of honey blonde. She might have been a pretty woman, but her face and lips were swollen into a horrific mask.

The things I could have done—that last-minute errand, martinis with Libba, the drive through the neighborhood to admire my neighbors' spring plantings—flashed through my brain. Heck, I could have swung by my parents' house for a cozy mother-daughter chat (one where Mother's disapproval of my choices was as tangible as her perfectly matched pearls). They were all better choices than coming home. To this.

I retreated till the back of my legs hit Henry's desk. I propped myself against its solid edge and blotted out the sight of Mrs. Anarchy Jones by pressing a palm against my eyes.

"Aggie!"

"Yes, ma'am?"

I shifted my palm a smidge and peeked. Aggie stood in the doorway holding a tray.

The hand not glued to my forehead clutched the coffee mug tighter than a drowning man held a life preserver. "She's dead."

"She can't be." Aggie shook her head, and orange curls sproinged in every direction. "She only arrived twenty minutes ago." Solid logic, but fatally flawed.

"Take a look," I suggested.

Aggie entered, deposited the coffee tray on Henry's desk, and observed the body—the face. "You're right. She's dead."

"I'm aware."

"Anarchy's a widower."

I blew out a slow breath. "She's not his wife. She can't be."

"Mom?" Grace, home from school with her backpack slung over her shoulder, appeared in the open doorway. "What are you doing in here?"

I pushed away from the desk. Grace had dealt with enough over the past year. Her plate was full. Adding another body was a terrible idea. "Nothing."

Her gaze landed on the one thing I didn't want her to see.

"I'm sorry. I didn't realize you had a guest." Her eyes narrowed. "Is she okay?"

Grace would figure out there was a problem when the police arrived. Hiding the body (the third in a year) in the study would never work. "She's dead."

The heavy backpack thunked to the floor. "Again?"

I nodded and went to her.

Grace's gaze searched my face, then returned to the woman in the chair. "Was she murdered?"

"I don't know." No visible blood, no wounds, no weapon—but given my record, chances were good.

"Why is she here?"

"I don't know."

"What's her name?"

I swallowed. "She told Aggie her name was—" I rubbed the back of my neck where tension threatened to snap tendons "—Mrs. Anarchy Jones."

Grace rolled her eyes. "Yeah, right."

"That's what she told me." Aggie held up the coffee mug I'd abandoned on Henry's desk. "More?"

"Please." With the warm comfort of a full mug, I pushed away from the desk.

Grace crossed her arms. "Whoever she is—was—she lied. Anarchy's not married. Have you called him?"

"Not yet."

"He'll want to know."

I walked to the doorway, glanced at the suitcases that would miss the flight to Italy, and sighed. "You're right. You're right."

"So call him."

The front door opened, a chill permeated the foyer, and Mother stepped inside. The wind hadn't dared touch the silver helmet of her hair. Her pumps, her lavender tweed suit, and the

Hermés scarf at her neck meant she'd come from a committee meeting or tea. Her gaze landed on me. "Oh, good. I caught you. I brought a list."

"A list?"

"Things you need to pick up for me in Italy." Her eyes narrowed. "Why are you lurking in a doorway?"

I tilted my head and stared at the chandelier hanging from the foyer's ceiling. The crystals cast rainbows on the crown molding.

"Ellison?"

If I pulled myself together, she might leave. "What, Mother?"

"What are you doing?" she demanded.

I swallowed. "Nothing."

"That response didn't work when you were fifteen. It doesn't work now."

Because it was her granna, Grace refrained from rolling her eyes. "Never works for me either."

She should have remained silent. Mother shifted her gaze. "They let you wear that to school?"

"Everyone wears jeans."

"If everyone jumped off the Empire State Building, would you do that, too?" Mother was in a mood. "Ellison, you let her out of the house in that?"

"Mother—" the forced smile curving my lips hid brittle self-control "—why don't you give me your list?"

Her eyes slitted. "You're hiding something."

"Me?" Too bad my voice squeaked.

She brushed past us, peeked into the study, and stopped dead. "You have company?"

"Not exactly."

Mother ventured into the study. "I'm sorry, I didn't realize —" she stiffened and looked back at me "—is she...?"

I nodded. "She's dead."

"Oh, Ellison." Mother pressed the pads of her fingers to her temples. "How could you?"

How could I what? Find a body? Why was she surprised? I found bodies all the time.

"Who is she?" Mother demanded.

"Not sure."

"Now strangers are coming to your house to die?"

The question hung in the air like a dialog bubble in the funnies.

"She told Aggie her name was Mrs. Anarchy Jones." Grace's doubt-filled tone made her opinion clear—the dead woman had lied.

"I knew it!" Mother jumped immediately to the dead-woman-was-telling-the-truth side of the fence, the Anarchy-Jones-is-a-huge-mistake side of the fence. In Mother's perfect world, I'd date a doctor or lawyer (preferably Hunter Tafft) or CEO. Having her daughter date a homicide detective did not fit her plan. "I knew you couldn't trust that man!"

"Anarchy is innocent till proven guilty." Somehow, I kept my voice mild. But inside, a more strident voice demanded I smack Mother upside the head.

"There's an easy way to find her name," said Grace.

"Check her wallet," said Aggie.

"Maybe Anarchy killed her." Mother sounded almost hopeful.

"That woman is not Anarchy's wife, and he didn't kill her." I'd had enough Mother to last till summer's end, and it hadn't arrived yet.

"Have you called him?" Mother demanded.

"Not yet."

"Why not?"

Because as soon as I picked up the phone, my Italian vacation would disappear faster than a gin martini at the nineteenth hole. "I'll call now." I crossed to Henry's desk, picked up the receiver, and hesitated.

"What are you waiting for, Mom?"

Arrivederci to gondola rides down the Grand Canal, sipping bellinis at Harry's Bar, visiting a vineyard in Tuscany, and shopping on the *Quadrilatero d'Oro*.

Arrivederci to Anarchy and me without murder, or mayhem, or my family. I let my Italian dream fade away and dialed.

"Jones."

"It's me."

"Hi." The warmth in his voice curled my toes. "Ready?"

So ready. "About that...um..."

"What's happened?" He sounded almost resigned, as if he'd been expecting disaster.

I closed my eyes. "There's a body in the study."

For long seconds, the silence from the other end of the phone line blared in my ear.

"Are you and Grace okay?"

"We're fine."

"Don't touch anything. I'm on my way."

I hung up the phone. Slowly. "Everybody out."

"Pardon?" Mother didn't appreciate being told what to do.

"Let's sit in the living room." I picked up the coffee tray from the desk and walked toward the door.

"There's a body." No flies on Mother.

"Yes," I agreed.

She tilted her head. "And you're taking coffee in the living room?"

"Anarchy asked us not to touch anything." If the mysterious dead woman had been murdered—given my track record, I assumed the worst—we'd probably trampled any clues. "He's on his way."

Mother sniffed.

Grace sneezed.

Aggie backed out of the room. "I'll start a fresh pot."

Coffee. The answer to so many of life's questions. "Thank you, Aggie."

Grace and Mother followed me to the living room, where Mother chose the corner of my new couch. Her fingers stroked the damask cloth, and her lips pursed. "Did you know he was married?"

"That's not his wife."

She raised her left brow. "Are you sure?"

I'd made the hard decision to trust Anarchy (no easy feat after my husband cheated with such reckless abandon). I wouldn't second guess my choice. Not without hard evidence. "Quite sure."

"Anarchy would never lie to Mom." Grace's confidence warmed my heart.

"Then who is she?" Mother stared at me as if she expected an immediate answer.

"I've never seen her before."

"Fresh coffee's on." Aggie stood in the doorway. "And I brought cookies."

Grace rose from the couch, claimed the cookie plate and a stack of napkins, and offered a cookie to her grandmother.

"No thank you, dear. I'm watching my waistline."

Grace waved the plate under my nose.

"Don't mind if I do." I selected a chocolate chip cookie and accepted a napkin.

"How can you eat when there's a corpse in the study?" Mother asked.

"If I stopped eating whenever I found a body, I'd starve."

Mother's mouth opened, but no words came out.

Grace put the cookie plate on the coffee table, helped herself to two cookies, and plopped onto the couch. "I wonder who she is."

"I wonder why she's here," I replied.

"I wonder what I did to deserve a daughter who stumbles over bodies so often she can be flippant about death."

Mother had half a point. I should be upset by the body in the study. The poor woman had died alone in a stranger's house. She probably had loved ones who'd mourn her passing. And, if those loved ones were local, I'd feel obligated to show up on their doorstep with a Bundt cake. I knew those things. But I didn't feel them. Not when my brain repeated the same question. Again and again. Why had she told Aggie she was Anarchy's wife?

There was no sadness till I had an answer.

"Pansy!" Aggie's voice carried from the kitchen.

Next came the distinctive click of claws on hardwood floors. Claws moving at an impressive clip. After that, the sound of Aggie's pursuit.

"Mother—"

My warning came too late. Pansy flew through the door to the living room and launched herself onto the couch.

It was too bad yesterday's shower had created pockets of mud in the backyard. It was a crying shame Pansy had wallowed in them. It was a tragedy she landed in Mother's lap.

For five horrible seconds, time stood still.

Then Mother shoved the dog to the floor. "Ellison Walford Russell!"

Ding, dong.

Pawprints and mud dotted Mother's Chanel suit. Anger flushed her cheeks. She stood. She glowered. At me. At the dog (who helped herself to a cookie from the coffee table). Even at

Aggie. Her head circled like Linda Blair's in *The Exorcist* (not really). "That beast must go."

"She's scheduled for sleepaway obedience training later in the week." I glanced toward the hall. "I'll just grab the door."

Answering the door might be a coward's escape, but it meant Mother's glare couldn't melt the skin from my bones. I nearly knocked Aggie over in my dash to the foyer.

I reached the front door, closed my fingers around the handle, and yanked it open.

Anarchy stood on my front stoop. Concern crinkled the skin around his coffee-colored eyes. Worry creased his forehead. "I heard yelling. Is everything okay?"

A hysterical giggle bubbled in my chest. "Pansy. Mother."

"Oh." A smile tugged at his lips. "That sounds bad."

"Awful." I glanced over my shoulder. "The body's in the study."

"The dog's?"

"No. Mother hasn't killed her. Yet. They're in the living room. The woman's body is in the study."

"Who is she?"

Oh dear. "I didn't talk to her. She told Aggie her name was..."

Anarchy waited.

I swallowed a golf-ball-size lump. "She told Aggie her name was Mrs. Anarchy Jones."

Anarchy's eyes widened. "What?"

I nodded; a new lump made uttering another syllable impossible.

"I'm not married."

I swallowed the second lump. "Ex-wife?"

The crease in his forehead deepened. "Nope."

Grace appeared in the entrance to the living room. She'd wrapped both her hands around Pansy's collar and dragged the still-muddy dog toward the kitchen. Pansy struggled, her nails clicking madly on the floor. Clearly, she wanted to stay with Mother and the cookies. The dog had a death wish.

"Bad dog!" I shook my finger at the miscreant retriever.

She stopped struggling and grinned at me.

Next to me, Anarchy chuckled. "I'll take a look in the study."

I nodded. "I'd better deal with Mother."

"You could come with me."

Dead body or Mother? The choice was easy. I followed him into the study.

Anarchy crouched next to the body and stared into the woman's face. "I've never seen her before."

A tiny Doubting Thomas portion of my soul exhaled. "Me neither."

"Did she tell Aggie what she wanted?"

"Only that she wanted to see me." I nodded toward the handbag, a British tan Coach stewardess, and its spilled contents. "We didn't touch anything."

Anarchy pulled on a pair of gloves, opened the billfold, and found the woman's driver's license. "Her name is Monica Alexander."

Not Mrs. Anarchy Jones. "Never heard of her."

He stared at the body and his shoulders slumped. "I have to call this in."

"I know."

"I'm not sure we'll make our flight." He gazed into my eyes as if he regretted the missed bellinis at Harry's, the wine not sipped under a Tuscan sun, the boots still waiting for my credit card.

"We'll go." My throat thickened with regret. "Just not today."

He stood and stepped close to me.

I stared up into his eyes. Gold flecks lightened his coffee-brown irises.

The air between us crackled and warmed and shivered with portent.

"I'm sorry about this." His voice was velvet.

"Not your fault."

"I wanted time for us." His lips touched mine, and I relaxed into his strong arms.

"Ellison Walford Russell!" Mother's scandalized voice made me leap three feet into the air. "Are you making out over a corpse?"

Chapter Two

"Grace?" I called up the back stairs. "Are you ready?"

"It's a stupid rule." Grace thought no jeans allowed in the clubhouse was so last decade.

"I didn't make the rule." I didn't disagree with the no-jeans rule. I didn't share my opinion with my grumbling daughter.

She descended the stairs wearing a dress and platform loafers.

"You look nice."

She rolled her eyes so far back in her head she could probably see her behind. "Let's go."

I slung my handbag over my shoulder and called, "Aggie, we're leaving." The police had asked me endless questions, and I needed an escape from their no-way-an-innocent-woman-finds-this-many-bodies gazes (not even Anarchy's presence could dispel their suspicions.

Aggie was in the laundry room giving Pansy a much-needed bath. "I'll stay till they leave." They. The police. They were treating the body—Monica Alexander—as a suspicious death.

"Thank you."

Grace and I drove to the club, parked, and made our way inside, where the hostess led us to a table in the casual dining room.

There was an impressive crowd for a Wednesday. Or maybe it just seemed that way because my friend Daisy had so many children with her.

I stopped at her table and counted noses. She had two extra.

She spotted me and her forehead wrinkled. "Aren't you supposed to be on a plane?"

"There's been a change in plans."

Her gaze filled with concern. "Is everything okay?"

Seven pairs of eyes stared at me. Eight if I counted Daisy's. "I'll tell you later. Who do you have with you tonight?"

"Billy and Robbie Sandhurst. Their sister is sick, and Lucinda has reached the end of her rope."

I smiled at the tow-headed Sandhurst boys, who sat at the table with their napkins and hands in their laps (Daisy's children bounced and shifted and poked and made horrible faces). "Looks as if you have your hands full."

Daisy raised a cocktail to her lips. "If you stab your sister with that fork, you can forget about seeing *The Apple Dumpling Gang*." She truly did have a hidden set of eyes.

Oh dear Lord. "I'll leave you to it." I joined Grace at our table, slid into my seat, and picked up the menu. "You should have said 'hello.'"

Grace shuddered. "She'd have asked me to babysit." She leaned forward and whispered, "They're monsters."

I hid my smile behind the menu. "What are you having?"

"A burger. And you're having a Cobb salad. Why do you bother looking?"

"You never know. I might try something different." I

ordered a Cobb salad every time we ate in the casual dining room.

"Ellison!"

I peeked over the top of my menu.

Jane Addison met my gaze. "I heard you found another body."

Heads swiveled. Jane didn't know the meaning of the word discreet.

I winced and nodded.

Grace stood. "Good evening, Mrs. Addison."

"Sit down, Grace." Jane waved at Grace's empty chair, waited till she sat, then demanded, "Who died?"

"I didn't know her."

"A she? I heard the throat was ripped out."

One of my neighbors had an active imagination.

"No." My fingers touched the pearls at my neck. "Do you honestly think I'd put on a twin set and come to dinner at the club if someone was butchered at my home?"

"Fair point." Jane sounded disappointed about the lack of gore. "Was she murdered?"

"It's an ongoing investigation. The police asked me not to comment." I'd always wanted to say that.

Jane tilted her head and frowned. "If you didn't know her, what was she doing at your house?"

"I wish I knew."

"How many bodies does that make?"

Around us, the remaining conversations screeched to a halt. Everyone in the dining room waited for my answer.

"I hate discussing murder over dinner." I cut my gaze toward Grace.

Behind Jane, a waiter cleared his throat. "May I get you anything to drink, Mrs. Russell?"

Was it warm enough for gin? After my afternoon, the

temperature outside didn't matter. "A gin and tonic, please. Two limes."

The waiter made a note. "And for you, miss?"

"Tab, please," said Grace. "I'd also like two limes."

"Right away." He left us.

I wished Jane would follow his lead, but her feet seemed rooted to the carpet. "You could sell the house." And she knew the perfect listing agent.

"I doubt anyone would want it." I wrinkled my nose. "All those murders."

"It's a double lot."

"I'm not selling, Jane."

She sighed. "Let me know if you change your mind."

"Promise." I smiled and returned my gaze to the menu (hint, hint).

"You're a giant poo-poo head!"

All eyes shifted away from me to Daisy's table (I owed one —possibly two—of Daisy's children an ice cream).

"Just you wait till your father gets home." It was Daisy's ultimate threat.

Momentarily cowed children stared at the white linen tablecloth with horrified expressions on their little faces.

"Nice seeing you, Ellison." Jane returned to her table, one close to Daisy's.

"See why I won't babysit?" Grace whispered.

"I see." Poor Daisy.

The waiter delivered our drinks, and I ordered a Cobb.

"A cheeseburger, please. With fries." Grace waited till the waiter left, then reached across the table and took my hand. "I'm sorry about your trip, Mom."

I took a long sip of gin. "There will be other trips."

"But you were totally looking forward to this one."

More than I could ever say. I squeezed Grace's hand. "I wish I knew what that woman wanted."

"Anarchy will figure it out." Her face clouded. "Why did she say she was his wife?"

"That's another question I'd love answered." I took another sip of gin. "How long till your grandmother forgives me?"

Grace covered a smile with her fingers. "You offered to pay for her dry cleaning."

"Pansy is staying with the obedience trainer till she learns some manners."

Grace's brows drew together, and her mouth turned down. "Max and I will miss her."

"Enough to walk her when we get home?"

She hunched her shoulders and scrunched her face into an insincere grin. "Homework."

That meant I was walking Pansy and Max. Ugh. I finished my drink in one sip.

PANSY AND MAX trotted at a moderate pace and pretended to be well-behaved dogs.

I wasn't fooled. Together, they outweighed me. Walking them required constant vigilance.

The soft night sent distractions. Squirrels. The scent of spring flowers. The creak of a porch swing. Owls. Debussy's "Claire de Lune" floated out an open window.

Pansy's freshly washed coat shined like gold in the streetlights, while Max's coat held a pewter sheen.

"I'm having a hard time mourning that woman's death," I admitted to the dogs. She'd lied about her name and died in my study. "I should be on a plane right now." I glanced at the night sky.

The dogs trotted onward.

"If she'd waited one day..." Aggie would have turned her away, and she could have died somewhere other than my late husband's study.

The dogs didn't care.

"I know I sound like a terrible person..."

Max glanced over his shoulder and grinned. It was a beautiful night. Why was I wallowing?

"Don't give me that look. Mother is furious. First, I found a body, then your girlfriend spoiled her suit."

Max returned his gaze to the sidewalk ahead.

It was Pansy's turn to grin over her shoulder.

Max tugged on his leash, and I tightened my hold. Ahead of us, a streetlight illuminated a man walking a dog—a Yorkie.

"Don't even think it." I pulled both dogs into the street. Max's attempts to pin miniature dogs with his giant paws often degenerated into a doggy version of Whac-A-Mole. "Hope Farmer hasn't spoken to me since you whapped her Pomeranian."

Max tugged harder.

"Nice night for a walk." The man stopped as if he hoped for a neighborly conversation.

Bad move.

Yip, yip, yip. His tiny dog was ready to battle my two behemoths.

Max and Pansy strained against my hold.

I kept walking. "Lovely evening. Hope you enjoy it."

Yip, yip, yip.

The little dog had a death wish—or it didn't understand size mattered.

I tugged on the dogs, who strained to follow the Yorkie.

They relented, and we walked onward. "You can't keep pinning dogs to the pavement, Max. Their owners don't like it."

He gave me a but-it's-fun glance, rubbed his shoulder against Pansy's, and picked up his pace.

"And don't you get naughty ideas, missy. You have plenty of bad habits already."

We walked another mile without incident. When our house came in view, I switched the leashes from my left hand to my right.

Pansy, sensing the lack of tension, pulled hard.

Her leash flew free. For a hopeful second, she paused. I dared to dream she'd let me pick up the leather strip and continue home.

I bent.

She ran.

Meow! A cat streaked through my neighbor's yard and disappeared around the corner of her house. Pansy followed.

"Was that Margaret's cat?" Dread weighted my voice.

Margaret Hamilton, my next-door neighbor who flew a broomstick whenever the moon was full, had a black cat (a familiar). The cat and Max had a long-standing feud. Now Pansy had picked a fight.

I tiptoed through Margaret's front lawn into her side yard and spotted Pansy.

Woof!

She'd stuck her head through the rungs of Margaret's wrought-iron fence. Presumably the cat was safely on the other side.

"Pansy!"

That got me a single tail wag.

"Leave that cat alone."

Woof!

"You're not catching the cat. Let's go."

Pansy's back legs reversed, but her head remained between the rungs.

Aaaarrrg.

It was the sound of a creature enduring unspeakable suffering.

"Are you stuck?"

Aaaarrrg. My new dog was a drama princess.

Woof! Save her!

"Max, that's not helpful." Any minute now, Margaret would appear and hex me into next year.

"Ellison?"

It was as if my thoughts had conjured her.

"What are you doing?"

I swallowed. "Pansy is stuck."

"Stuck?" Margaret (clad in black—as usual) exited her screened porch and joined me on the lawn. "How?"

"She chased your cat." A dangerous admission.

Margaret sniffed. "Serves her right." The neighbors regarded my decision to adopt Pansy, a dog known for digging craters in yards, shredding annuals, and causing mayhem, with extreme prejudice (I couldn't blame them—Pansy was a disaster on four paws).

"I can't leave her there."

Margaret sighed. "I suppose not. You can cut through the porch to the backyard."

"And?"

She cast an evil glance my way. "She got her head through the rungs. There must be a way to get her out."

Woof!

"Okay," I agreed. "But I'm taking Max home first."

Max did not want to leave his lady love with her head stuck in a fence. He dug in his paws, he resisted the leash, he tested my last nerve.

"I can't help her till you're home."

He didn't believe me.

"Max, trust me." Something in my voice sank into his doggy brain, and he whined softly. "I know you're worried. Let's go."

We hurried across my lawn, and I unlocked the front door and shoved a still-reluctant Max through it. Then I took a deep breath and returned to Margaret and Pansy.

"One ill-mannered dog wasn't enough for you?"

Aaaarrrg.

"I apologize for this. I'll free her, and we'll be out of your hair."

"Hmph."

I cut through Margaret's porch (wicker furniture, plump cushions), exited into her backyard, and circled the house to the fence.

Pansy spotted me. *Aaaarrrg.*

"We'll get you out." I sounded more confident than I felt. How had she got her head through the fence? Her noggin was obviously larger than the space between the rungs.

I crouched next to her. "Can you turn your head?"

Aaaarrrg.

"Calm down, Pansy." I went for the same soothing tone I'd used on Max.

Aaaarrrg.

It was obvious Pansy's back legs still worked to free her. The tension against the iron rungs pushed her ears and cheeks forward.

"Can you turn your head?" I asked.

Pansy gave me the equivalent of a doggy eye roll.

"Just asking." I put my hands on her forehead and chin and angled her head. "This might work. Can you pull?"

"Me?" Margaret replied. "Are you kidding?"

"Please?"

Gently I angled Pansy's head. Margaret pulled (on what I didn't ask). Pansy remained stuck.

Aaaarrrg.

"You shoved your head through." I scratched behind Pansy's ear. "How?"

"Leave her. We'll call the fire department in the morning."

Aaaarrrg. Pansy didn't care for that idea. At all.

"That would be cruel."

The hex Margaret was planning for me skittered down my spine.

"Have you ever had a ring stuck on your finger?" she asked.

"Everyone has."

"How did you get it off?"

"Soap." I regarded the dog and the narrow rungs. "I don't think soap will work."

"The principle."

"You have another idea?"

"I do." Margaret cackled.

That cackle sent ice shards through my bloodstream.

"I'll be right back." The door to the screen porch opened, and Margaret left me alone with my dog.

"We'll get you out. I promise." And hopefully the spell Margaret used to turn Poppy into a toad wouldn't last long. I gazed into her worried eyes. "Learn from your mistakes. Don't chase cats. Don't stick your head through fences."

Woof. What's the fun in a life half-lived?

"Here." Margaret joined me on the head side of the fence and handed me a bottle.

"Wesson oil?"

"You have a better idea?"

Dare I suggest we remove a rung? I bit my lip and took the bottle.

Margaret crossed her arms. "Someone died at your house today?"

"Yes."

"Never a dull moment with you as a neighbor." She sounded almost amused.

"I'd welcome dull," I replied. "No murder, no doggy destruction."

"You had dull."

"Pardon?"

"How long have we been neighbors?"

"Almost twenty years."

"For almost twenty years, you were dull. You let your husband hide your light. Now that he's gone, you shine." She grinned "And interesting things happen."

Aaaarrrg. As the current interesting thing, Pansy wanted help.

I stroked her forehead and allowed myself a moment to think. Had Henry purposefully—as Margaret said—hid my light? Or had we both settled into expectations? The man brought home the bacon. The woman fried it up in a pan (metaphorically speaking. I couldn't fry bacon if my life depended on it).

I sat back on my heels.

Henry and I started our life together certain we'd soar. Instead, we'd thudded to hard-packed earth.

"As your neighbor, I miss dull."

I bet she did. I held up the bottle. "What do we do with this?"

"You pour it over her head. And push. I'll go to the other side and pull."

"She just had a bath."

"Give her another one."

I glanced at the rungs. "We could—"

A fierce expression settled on Margaret's face. "Destroying my fence is a last resort."

"Okay." My voice was meek. We'd try the oil. I unscrewed

the cap and dribbled a few drops on Pansy's head.

Pansy's gaze followed the bottle. *Woof! Seriously?*

"It will take more than that." Margaret rubbed her pointy chin. "Also, unhook her collar. She might have an easier time getting through without it."

No collar meant no leash. "That might not be the best—"

"I have no intention of spending the night out here with you and this beast."

I unhooked Pansy's leash.

"The collar, Ellison."

This was a bad idea. I removed Pansy's collar.

"Let me get to the front yard, then pour." She cut through the porch. "Ready."

"Sorry about this," I whispered.

Pansy whined softly.

I poured.

"Get behind her ears," Margaret advised.

I poured oil behind Pansy's ears, on the top of her head, around her cheeks. Then I put the bottle in the grass and gently turned her head. "Back up, girl."

She tried. Hard. But she remained stuck.

"You need more oil," Margaret advised.

We needed a fireman with a saw capable of cutting iron. I kept that thought to myself and poured more oil.

"Now try."

I turned Pansy's head. Margaret grabbed her haunches. Pansy whined. And miraculously her head slipped through the rungs.

Pansy flew backward and flattened Margaret.

"Oomph."

Before I could ask if Margaret was okay, Pansy shook her head. Oil flew around her like a garden sprinkler. Then she struggled to get up. There were oily paws, and oily fur, and oily whiskers everywhere—or that's what Margaret's choice words described.

"Pansy! Sit!"

The fence between us diluted my almost nonexistent authority. Worse, Pansy's collar was clutched in my hand. She scrabbled free of Margaret and ran as if a witch might blast off her tail.

I dashed through the porch and crouched next to Margaret. "Are you hurt?"

"I'll live. I can't speak for that dog."

"She's leaving for obedience training on Friday." I hefted Margaret off her prone position on the trampled grass. "I promise." Where had Pansy gone? I scanned my front yard. She was capable of enormous destruction—flowers, sod, hostas. "I should find her."

"Go." Margaret waved me away.

I hurried toward my own yard.

"Ellison." Margaret stopped me with a word. "If I see that dog in my yard again, she won't like the consequences."

Yikes. I had fresh visions of Pansy as a toad, or a spare broomstick, or an actual pansy. "I understand."

"Also—" Here came the part where she turned me into a toad or a pansy.

"Yes?"

"I lied. I like you better now that you shine."

Chapter Three

Pansy ran as if hell hounds nipped at her heels.

I wasn't a hell hound, and I was nowhere near her heels.

She blurred to a blonde streak as she raced across the street, dashed through the Dixons' hedge, and sprinted toward the bottom of the hill.

"Pansy!" If she ran into the road, a car might hit her.

I regularly jogged laps around Loose Park, but sprinting was new. The sudden stitch in my side nearly brought me to my knees. I stumbled to a halt, raised my right arm in the air, and leaned to the left. I gasped for air.

Meanwhile, Pansy extended the distance between us.

I ignored the stabbing pain under my ribs and hobbled after her. "Pansy!"

Either she didn't hear me (people in the next state heard me), or she was an expert in situational deafness. She disappeared around the corner.

Screech! A car's tires objected to the sudden application of brakes.

My heart, already beating double-time, stopped. I flew

toward the bottom of the hill. Pansy! Tears welled in my eyes. *Please let her be okay. Please let her be okay.* How would I ever explain her loss to Grace? To Max?

I rounded the corner.

Pansy (miraculously in one piece) stood in front of a car.

A man—the man—held her by the scruff of the neck.

She wagged her tail as if she'd planned her near-miss and rescue.

"Lose someone?" asked Anarchy.

I battled for breath and lost. Rather than answer, I leaned forward and rested my forearms on my knees.

"Are you okay?" Concern softened the edges of his voice.

I held up a hand. I needed thirty seconds for the stitch in my side to ease, my heart rate to return to human levels, and my lungs to re-inflate.

"Do you have her collar?"

Pansy's collar remained clutched in my hand. I held it up like a trophy. Her leash lay forgotten in the grass at Margaret's.

"Sit," said Anarchy.

Pansy sat.

"Stay."

Pansy stared at him with adoring eyes.

Anarchy walked toward me, and Pansy stayed.

He took the collar from my hand, then buckled the pink leather strip around her neck. "Why is she oily?"

I drew air into my lungs and held it. "She got herself stuck in a fence."

"And you used oil to get her out?"

"It was Margaret's idea." I glared at Pansy. She had my wrath to deal with, plus the lingering threat of Margaret's hex.

"Let's get her home."

I held Pansy's collar (death grip was too lax a description for my hold) and Anarchy pulled his car to the curb.

Anarchy took control of Pansy (she wriggled with happiness) and together, we walked her to my house.

"What's in the bag?" I asked.

Anarchy carried a paper sack in the arm he wasn't using to hold Pansy. "A surprise."

"I'm not sure I can withstand another surprise."

"It's a good one."

"What is it?"

His white grin flashed like a beacon in the night. "You'll see."

We reached my yard, walked up the drive, and bypassed the front door.

"I don't want her in the house. She needs a bath." Pansy's oily fur, left unattended, had the power to destroy half my upholstery. I envisioned hefting her into a bathtub, attaching the spray hose to the faucet, and dousing her in shampoo. My nose wrinkled with anticipated wet-dog aroma.

"Do it later."

"Later?"

"Surprise first, bath later." Anarchy gently pushed me into a chair on the patio. "I'll be right back."

I tilted my head and stared at the stars. Anarchy disappeared into the kitchen. Max dashed outside and checked on Pansy's welfare.

"You two are lucky I'm soft-hearted."

The dogs grinned at me, then settled on patio next to each other. I closed my eyes.

"For you." Anarchy offered me a Champagne glass.

"What's this?"

"A bellini." He took the chair next to mine.

"You made bellinis?"

"Since we can't get to Italy, I brought you a taste of Venice."

Tears swam in my eyes. "Thank you."

We touched the rims of our glasses, and I sipped peach juice and prosecco.

"Have you been to Harry's Bar?" Anarchy asked.

"Yes."

"What's it like?"

"Small. Six barstools and seating for thirty. Lots of butter-scotch-colored wood. The waiters and the bartender wear white jackets and black bowties."

"Let's pretend we're there." It was official—Anarchy Jones was a romantic.

If I wasn't already in love with him, the bellinis, the moon-light, and the thoughtfulness would have pushed me over the edge. "This. Right here. Right now. My patio. Pansy covered in oil. You. It's perfect. I wouldn't change a thing."

Anarchy reached for my hand. Our fingers touched. We smiled at each other.

"We will get to Italy, Ellison. I promise."

"I'll hold you to that." If we didn't change the subject, I'd swoon at his feet. "What have you learned about Monica Alexander?"

He rubbed the back of his neck. "We're waiting on the autopsy."

That would supply cause of death without answering the bigger question. "Why would a woman neither of us have seen before show up at my house and claim to be your wife? How did someone I've never seen before know to use your name? Is she from Kansas City?"

He shook his head. "No."

That only made things stranger. "San Francisco?" It made sense. The woman—Monica—had claimed to be Anarchy's wife, and he moved to Kansas City from the Bay Area. Maybe she lurked forgotten in his past.

"Lake Forest, Illinois."

"Really?" I knew people in Lake Forest. Lots of them. "Chip Robertson lives in Lake Forest."

"Who?"

"A friend from art school. He runs an ad agency now. If she's from Lake Forest, I'd bet money he knows her. He knows everyone."

A frown creased Anarchy's forehead. "How big is Lake Forest?"

I considered my answer. "Probably fifteen thousand. Everyone belongs to the same clubs, eats in the same restaurants, supports the same charities—"

"Like here."

"Yes and no."

"Oh?"

"We're less insulated."

Anarchy refrained—somehow—from rolling his eyes.

"Lake Forest is like Nob Hill with more land," I explained Lake Forest in San Francisco terms. "I'll call Chip in the morning."

The crease in his forehead made another appearance. "Were you friends or did you date him?"

Was Anarchy jealous? I suppressed a smile. "Friends. Just friends."

"Call him."

"It's just so odd." I stared up at the stars. "Have you tracked down her next of kin?" They might know why she'd knocked on my door and lied to Aggie.

"We can't find them. We get a machine when we call her home number."

I finished my bellini and glanced at Anarchy's empty glass. "Shall I make the next round?"

He stood. "Let me."

I didn't argue—not after my mad dash through the neighborhood. I relinquished my glass, stretched my legs, and let my head fall against the back of the chair. What a day. A body. Jane Addison's nosy questions. Pansy's escapade. And a doggy bath still in my future. On the plus side, Anarchy. He far outweighed the negatives.

Voices—Anarchy's and Grace's—carried from the kitchen.

"Pansy ran away?" Grace stood at the screen door.

I opened one eye. "You could say that. She needs a bath."

"I'll bathe her."

"You will?"

"Sure. You look tired." Grace clapped her hands together. "Here, Pansy."

Pansy rose to her feet, yawned, and ambled to Grace. Max watched her go. As much as he adored Pansy, he hated baths.

Grace caught hold of Pansy's collar. "Granddad called."

"Oh?" My father wasn't one for calling.

"You're playing golf tomorrow. You have a two o'clock tee time."

"I am? I do?"

"Granna probably told him about the body."

"Safe bet." Daddy did his talking on the golf course. If he wanted to play with me rather than his usual cronies, he had an issue to discuss. *Ellison, I worry about you and the dead people.*

Grace let Anarchy squeeze past her, tightened her hold on Pansy's collar, and disappeared inside.

Anarchy handed me a fresh glass. "She's a great kid."

"I think so." I raised the glass's rim. "What shall we drink to?"

"To us."

Max lifted his head from his paws. *Woof!*

"Ellison?" Libba's voice floated through the screen.

If Anarchy and I ever had more than five minutes alone together, pigs would fly. "Patio," I called.

She appeared in the doorway wearing a draped satin jump-suit with a v-shaped neckline that reached her knees. She rested her hand on a jutted hip and stared at us (the overall effect was I-just-had-sex-and-now-I-need-a-cocktail). "Am I interrupting?"

Yes!

"I heard you found a body. I wanted to make sure you're okay."

"I'm fine." I couldn't be annoyed with her, not when she'd come to check on me.

"Where was it? The body?"

"In the study."

"If I were you, I'd padlock Henry's study."

My answering laugh walked a tightrope between amusement and tears. "That's not a bad idea."

"Murdered?"

"We're not sure," said Anarchy.

"A stranger." She joined us on the patio. "A woman. That's what I heard."

"Yes," I confirmed.

"Why did she die at your house? Did Frances arrange it to disrupt your trip?"

"Mother wouldn't do that." The logistics were too much for even Frances Walford.

"Pfft." Libba perused her seating choices before dropping into a chair next to the table we used when we dined *al fresco*. "What did the woman want?"

"We don't know."

She eyed our glasses. "What are you drinking?"

"Bellinis."

Libba winced as if she'd just realized she was inter-rupting. "Venice. Harry's Bar. Very romantic. Very delicious."

"If Ellison has more prosecco, I can make you one," Anarchy offered.

"I'd prefer a martini."

Anarchy stood. "Vodka or gin?"

"Surprise me but make it dry."

We watched him disappear into the house.

Libba lifted a brow. "He's playing host now?"

"I suppose he is."

"Sorry to interrupt your evening." She didn't sound remotely sorry.

"Oh?"

She clasped her hands in her lap. "I need to talk to you."

"What's wrong?"

She glanced at the door and leaned toward me. "It's about Jimmy." Jimmy was the much younger firefighter Libba dated.

"What about him?"

"He noticed I got my hair trimmed."

"It looks nice."

"Of course it does." She touched her tousled locks with the tips of her fingers. "That's not the point."

"Enlighten me."

"He told me he likes my hair longer."

"And?"

"That's how it starts." She sat back in her chair, dug a pack of cigarettes from her purse, and lit one.

I frowned. Had Libba downed a few martinis before she arrived? "How what starts?"

"He likes my hair longer."

"And?

"What if I like my hair shorter?"

"Then don't grow it out."

"But he likes it longer."

We were talking in circles. "It's your hair."

She exhaled an elegant plume of smoke. "What would you do if Anarchy asked you to change your hair?"

I stared at her. "Have you lost your mind?"

"It starts with hair."

"What? What starts?"

"Control."

"You think Jimmy's trying to control you?"

"Has Anarchy asked you to change your hair?"

"No."

"What about Ellison's hair?" Anarchy stepped onto the patio and handed Libba a martini.

"You haven't asked her to change it," Libba replied.

"It's her hair."

Libba lifted her martini glass as if she'd scored a point.

"Let me get this straight." Libba interrupted my evening for this? "You're upset because Jimmy doesn't like your haircut?"

She scowled at me. "You're missing the point."

"Obviously."

She drank deeply. "If I change my hair to please him, what's next? My clothes? My lipstick? My nail polish?" She parked her cigarette in the ashtray, held out her free hand, and admired her manicure. "Have you ever noticed that Myrna Green always wears red polish?"

I blinked.

"Do you think it's because Myrna likes red?"

I blinked again. I'd never noticed Myrna's nail polish.

"No." Libba stabbed a crimson nail my direction. "Myrna prefers pink. She wears red because her husband likes it."

I glanced at Anarchy. The poor man. Libba could be hard to follow at the best of times. Tonight was not the best of times.

"What I'm saying is we—women—make a million small concessions. Red nail polish, pink lipstick, the length of our hair, the length of our skirts—all to please a man. Those concessions add up!" She stabbed at me again. "Before you know it, you've changed so much you're not you!"

"Men make changes."

"Oh, please. They get married and learn to pick up their dirty underwear and, if their wives are lucky, put the toilet seat down when they're done."

Anarchy backed toward the door.

"What did Henry ever change for you?"

"Nothing."

"And you changed everything for Henry."

"Not everything."

She ceded my point with the tiniest of nods. "Almost everything. Now that he's gone, you're you." She cast her furious gaze toward Anarchy. "Don't you dare try and change her."

He held up his hands. "I wouldn't dream of it."

"Libba—" somehow, I kept my tone conversational "—do you think you might be overreacting?"

"Absolutely not. If Anarchy asked you to stop painting, would you?"

"No." My answer was immediate. Painting was an essential part of me.

"I'd never ask her that."

Libba rolled her eyes. "If Ellison asked you to quit your job, would you give up being a cop?"

"No."

"Same principle for a haircut." She stabbed out her cigarette.

Libba sometimes made some sense. Tonight she'd lost me completely.

"Mom." Grace appeared at the door. "You have a call."

Thank the Lord. "Who is it?"

"Mrs. Burkhart. She wants to know if you can sub for bridge tomorrow."

"I'm playing golf."

"That's what I told her. She said they play at ten. You'll be done in plenty of time to make your tee time."

If Grace had answered the phone in the kitchen, Liz Burkhart had just heard our exchange. I sighed and pushed out of my chair.

Inside, the receiver rested on the kitchen counter. I wrapped the stretched-to-near-breaking cord around my finger and pressed the phone to my ear. "Hello."

"Ellison, it's Liz. We need you! Please say you'll play with us tomorrow morning."

"I—"

"I know you don't have anything on your calendar. You're supposed to be in Italy."

I didn't need reminding. "I—"

"I'd be eternally grateful."

"Liz, someone died at my house today."

"When has that ever stopped you from playing bridge?"

She had a point.

"Fine. I'll be there." The manners Mother drilled into me took over. "Thank you for thinking of me."

"Thank you for subbing."

"My pleasure."

"Loser buys lunch."

Liz's husband had more money than God, and she played cards for her lunch tab? "Sounds fun. I'll see you tomorrow." I hung up the phone.

Outside, Libba harangued Anarchy about haircuts and women who compromised themselves to make men happy.

From the bathroom came the sound of running water. Grace muttered a word no mother wanted her daughter to use.

I pretended I didn't hear her. What disaster made her use

it? With Pansy it could be anything from an accidental soaking to flooding the bathroom.

I leaned against the counter and took a slow breath. Somewhere over the Atlantic was a plane with two empty first-class seats.

There would be other planes. Other trips. Other opportunities for Anarchy and me to escape.

I straightened my shoulders, lifted my chin, and returned to the patio.

"She told you she was Anarchy's wife?" Libba stared at me as if I were responsible for killing Monica.

"She told Aggie."

She shrugged. "Same difference."

"She was dead when I arrived."

Libba rested her elbow on the table's glass surface, then settled her chin onto her hand. She stared into the darkness as if answers hid in the shadows. "Mrs. Anarchy Jones. Why?"

"It's not as if we can ask her."

Anarchy took his beeper off his belt and frowned. "May I use the phone?"

"Of course." He didn't need to ask.

Libba watched him disappear inside. "Are you okay?"

"Fine. Why wouldn't I be?"

"You were looking forward to Italy."

"Italy will be there next week." Or next month. Or next year. Or whenever Anarchy and I managed to carve time out of our everyday lives.

"You never saw the woman before?"

"Never."

"Ellison." Anarchy's voice was too high.

I shifted my gaze to the house.

He stood framed by the light from the doorway. His hand clutched the door as if he needed its support.

I stood. "What's wrong?"

"I have to go."

"Another murder?"

He winced. "Not yet."

Libba polished off her martini and lit another cigarette. "This sounds interesting. What's happened?"

Anarchy released the door frame and rubbed his palm over his eyes.

"My mother."

I rose from my chair. "Is she all right?"

"She's fine." Now his palm covered his mouth. "Sheesear."

"What?"

He glanced at the stars, at Libba, at Max—anywhere but me. "She's here."

"Here?" I squeaked.

"In Kansas City. It's a surprise visit. She wants to meet you."

Chapter Four

I rested my elbows on the kitchen island and stared at Mr. Coffee. "What would I do without you?"

He winked—a saucy, yellow-gingham wink. That wink was as good as a promise. He'd remain by my side forever. Enduring life apart was unthinkable.

I took an enormous sip of coffee and offered him a doting smile. We were alone and he was an excellent secret-keeper. "His mother wants to meet me." The quaver when I said "mother" revealed my nerves.

She'll love you. Mr. Coffee was great at reassuring me. *You're beautiful and talented and have excellent taste.*

"You're just saying that because I love coffee." I wrapped my hands around the coffee mug, glad of its warmth. What if Mrs. Jones didn't love me? What if she didn't like me?

What kind of woman flew halfway across the country as a surprise? If Monica Alexander hadn't died in the study, Mrs. Jones would have arrived and found her son gone.

Yet another reason to mourn the trip to Italy.

"Mom!" Grace's voice tumbled down the back stairs. "Have you seen my jean jacket with the rainbow?"

"Did you hang it up?"

"No."

"If you hung it up, you'd know where it is." Oh dear Lord. I was becoming Mother. "I'll look in the den." I tightened my hold on my coffee mug and whispered to Mr. Coffee, "I'll be back."

Mr. Coffee already knew that. I was only on my first cup.

Grace's jacket draped over the couch's arm. The jacket was a gift from Aunt Sis (Mother's globe-trotting sister who'd recently married her high-school sweetheart). The jacket was a work of art. The rainbow traveled from the left cuff, over the left shoulder, did a loop on the back, stretched around the right front, and ended at the placket. It wasn't just a denim jacket; it was Grace's latest prized possession. I grabbed it, picked up my address book from my desk, and returned to the kitchen. "Found it," I called.

Grace's steps clattered down the stairs.

I winced at the sharp clacking made by wood heels meeting wood floor treads. Baretraps or Dr. Scholl's?

She burst through the door, and I glanced at her feet.

Baretraps. Platform sandals. She'd paired them with a floaty dress.

"You look nice."

"Thanks." She held out her hand for the jacket and put it on.

"Breakfast?" I asked. Aggie had left a plate of blueberry muffins on the counter.

"I'll take one to go." Grace hefted her backpack and handbag over her right shoulder and grabbed a muffin.

"Thanks for bathing Pansy."

"You're wecum." She'd filled her mouth with muffin.

"Seeyalater." She pushed open the back door and disappeared into the morning sunshine.

I refilled my coffee cup, gave Mr. Coffee a grateful pat, sat down at the island, and helped myself to a muffin. The wrapper peeled easily, and I took an enormous bite. Aggie baked like a dream—the tartness of the blueberries and sweetness of the cake brought a moan to my lips.

Mr. Coffee lifted a brow.

"So good with coffee." It wouldn't do to make him jealous.

Part of me (most of me) wanted to take my coffee back to bed, hide under the covers, and pretend Anarchy's mother wasn't in Kansas City. Instead, I turned pages in my address book. My fingers traced R names till I found Chip's number.

I glanced at the kitchen clock.

A quarter to eight. Too early to call his home. But not his office. I might get lucky and catch him.

I went to the phone and dialed.

"Robertson, Bills." The woman who answered the phone sounded put together, professional, ready to conquer the day.

I brushed a muffin crumb off my robe. "Chip Robertson, please."

"Please hold while I connect you with his assistant."

I took a quick sip of coffee.

"Mr. Robertson's office. How may I help you?"

"May I please speak with Chip?"

"I'm sorry. He's not available at the moment."

Too bad. A chat with Chip would be a welcome distraction from the specter of Anarchy's mother. "May I leave a message?"

"Of course. Your name, please?"

"Ellison Russell. Will he be in soon?"

"Mr. Robertson has client meetings most of the day."

"Please ask him to call me." I gave her my number.

"May I ask what this is regarding?"

"Chip and I are friends."

She paused as if she didn't believe me, as if I were some homewrecker calling Chip at work to avoid speaking with his wife.

"We went to art school together," I added.

She sniffed. "I'll give Mr. Robertson the message."

"Thank you." I hung up the phone and topped off my coffee.

The muffins called to me—*Ellison. One more.* That was the problem with Aggie's baking—resisting cakes and muffins and cookies was almost impossible.

Ignoring their siren call, I dropped six muffins into a decorative tin I scrounged from the cupboard. They'd be a gift for Margaret. An apology for Pansy's shenanigans. And Margaret, who was bony and knobby and sharp-edged, could afford the calories.

Before I headed to the club, I dropped them with her housekeeper.

The clock the on the dashboard read five minutes till ten when I pulled into the parking lot. I scanned for the best parking spot. Too close to other cars and someone could hide and ambush me. Too far from the clubhouse and no one might hear my cries for help (the club parking lot was almost as dangerous as Henry's study). I found a suitable spot and, at exactly ten o'clock, breezed into the card room.

Liz, Ainslie, and Cynthia were already seated.

"Am I late?"

"You're right on time," Liz assured me. "Thanks again for subbing."

I hooked my handbag over the back of the empty chair and took the seat across from Liz. "My pleasure."

"So sorry about your trip." Ainslie patted the hand I'd rested on the table.

"Such a horrible reason to postpone," said Cynthia.

"Awful," I agreed.

"The body was in the study?" Cynthia hooked me with the sharpness of her curious gaze. "Isn't that where Khaki died?"

"Yes." I spoke through stiff lips. If we spent the morning discussing the people who'd died at my house, I'd need to drink my lunch. "Shall we play?"

We drew for deal.

Ainslie won and dealt.

"Who was it?" Cynthia watched her partner deal. "The dead person?"

"Her name was Monica Alexander. She's from Lake Forest. That's all I know." Forestalling their curiosity was an impossibility, but I had to try.

"Lake Forest? Illinois?" Cynthia raised a sculpted brow. "My college roommate was from Lake Forest."

Liz frowned. "Isn't that where the executives from Al Winston's Chicago company live?"

"How could you remember that?" Ainslie dealt herself the last card.

"It's why Helen needed a sub. Al sprung a dinner party on her. He flew the executives in for a meeting. Their wives came, too."

We collected our cards in stacks, but I put off looking at mine. "Liz, we haven't played together in a while. Do you play a weak two?"

She nodded. "A weak three means I have seven."

"Jacoby?"

She nodded. "And stamen."

I looked at my hand. Fifteen points and even distribution. Good thing we'd discussed conventions.

"Pass," said Ainslie.

I recounted my points. Sixteen with even distribution. "One no-trump."

Cynthia scowled at her cards. "Pass."

"Two clubs." That bid meant Liz held at least one four-card major.

Ainslie passed.

I held four spades. Three of them face cards. "Two spades."

"Pass," said Cynthia.

"Three spades." Liz was giving me the choice—three no-trump or four spades.

I considered asking for aces but reaching for slam when I wasn't familiar with my partner's bidding was risky. "Four spades."

Cynthia led the two of clubs, and Liz put down the dummy hand.

I took a moment. Liz had the missing face card in spades and ten points. I needed to finesse for the king of diamonds, and we'd lose a heart trick. Other than that, making game was easy. I played quickly, glad to think about cards instead of murder or Anarchy's mother.

We made six.

"How could we have bid that better?" asked Liz.

"We fit," I replied as Cynthia cut for me.

"Are you rescheduling your trip?" Ainslie lifted her coffee cup to her lips.

Where was the waiter? Coffee might help me field all these questions. I gave a noncommittal shrug. "I'm sure we will." As soon as possible. Maybe tomorrow.

Ainslie sighed and leaned against the back of her chair. "I think it's marvelous that you're running away to Italy with that man."

The cards I was dealing stuttered, sending one wide. That man. Anarchy. "We're not running away. Just a vacation."

"Everything's fresh. And new. And exciting." Ainslie sighed as if she was imagining herself crossing the Ponte di Rialto. "It's romantic. It's not like traveling with your husband, where you know you'll be arguing over how much to tip the bellhop or whether to go to a museum or shopping."

"The last time Randal and I took a trip together, just the two of us—" Liz gazed out the window at the verdant golf course "—we went hiking in Tuscany."

"And?" Cynthia tilted her head as if she knew there was more to the story.

"I came home so exhausted I had to book myself into a week at a resort."

"You're the only person I know who needs a vacation from vacationing."

"You haven't traveled with Randal."

I picked up my cards and sorted by suit. "One heart."

"One spade," said Cynthia.

Liz eyed her cards and pursed her lips. "Pass."

"Three spades."

I took a second look at my hand. I was void in spades. "Pass."

"Four spades." Cynthia rapped her cards closed against the table's edge.

Liz led me a heart, and Ainslie laid the dummy hand on the table.

I took the trick with the ace of hearts, watched Liz sweep the cards, and led her the king.

Liz sloughed a diamond, watched Cynthia play a low heart from the board, and swept again.

As dummy, Ainslie watched. "Did you hear what Stuart Crane did to Jackie?"

"What?" I led the two of hearts.

"You know about their ugly divorce?"

"Everyone knows about their divorce." Cynthia played the jack from her hand.

Liz trumped with the two of spades. "What did Stuart do?"

Cynthia sighed and played the lowest heart from the board. "That's enough of that."

Ainslie studied the cards still on the table. "Jackie got the house."

Liz swept the trick and played the ace of clubs. "And?"

Cynthia groaned and played a low club from the table. I pitched a nine (the highest card I could afford to lose).

"She gave him a day to remove his things."

Liz lifted her brows and led a low club.

I took the trick with the king of clubs. "What happened?"

"He went through the whole house with Super Glue. The phone was glued to the cradle. The silverware was glued in the drawer. The oven mitts were glued to the wall." Ainslie shook her head as if she had no idea how she and Cynthia had bid so high. That or she was mourning Jackie's oven mitts.

I led another heart.

Again, Liz trumped and won the trick.

"That's enough of that," Cynthia grumbled.

Liz led a diamond, and Cynthia's expression cleared.

Cynthia won the trick in her hand and led a spade. "Speaking of houses, you'll appreciate this, Ellison. Helen and Al Winston loaned Prudence Davies their lake house."

"Oh?" I considered the cards in my hand, kept my voice neutral, and pitched a diamond.

"That's not the story." A wicked smile touched Cynthia's lips. "She left the place a mess and gave them a vase as a thank-you gift."

"She left it a mess?" Who did that?

"That's not the good part of the story."

"Did she Super Glue their kitchen?" asked Liz.

Cynthia's eyes sparkled. "A few weeks ago, Helen made her donation to the Junior League Thrift Shop." A membership requirement for us all, and an annual reason to clean closets.

I sensed where this was going. "She didn't."

"She did." Cynthia's smile was pure sunshine. "Prudence gave Helen the vase she'd donated."

"How did Helen know?"

"She's incredibly observant, and there was a chip near the base she recognized."

We played till noon, then Ainslie, who'd lost in a big way, signed for our lunches (four Cobb salads with dressing on the side, two iced teas, an Arnold Palmer, and a Perrier). We chatted, ate our salads, and declined dessert.

Ainslie glanced at her watch. "Girls, I must run. I have a hair appointment."

"What time is it?" asked Cynthia.

"Half past one."

Cynthia gasped and pushed out of her chair. "Ellison, thanks for playing. Lovely to see you." She swung her handbag over her shoulder. "I must fly."

I started to rise, but Liz touched my hand. "Do you have time for coffee?"

"I do." There was no point in going home. Not when I was due back here at two. Plus—coffee.

The waiter brought two cups.

Liz added sugar.

I added cream.

Liz stirred and caught her lower lip in her teeth, the very picture of a woman about to ask a favor.

I waited and prayed she wouldn't ask me to chair an event, lead a committee, or join a club.

She kept her gaze on her coffee cup. "I have a question..."

Here it came. I prepared an apologetic no.

"Before Henry died, did you consider divorce?"

That was her question? "I did."

Were Liz and Randal having trouble?

"Do you mind being alone?"

Liz and Randal were having trouble.

"I'd rather be alone than—" I wasn't alone "—than with Henry."

"You're dating."

"Yes."

"Is it awful?"

"Nerve-wracking, but not awful." The opposite of awful. Dating Anarchy was the stuff dreams were made of.

"You and the detective—"

"Anarchy," I supplied.

"That's right." She nodded. "You like him."

"I do." Understatement of the decade.

She gazed into her coffee cup as if it held the answers to her questions. "You know how relationships are like oceans?"

"Um..."

"Waves and troughs."

I nodded.

"Randal and I have been in a trough forever. We're roommates with children. I want more than that."

"Divorce is ugly."

She nodded. "And there are the children to think of. Is it fair for me to upend their lives because I miss fireworks? Because I want more?" She pressed her hand to her lips as if she couldn't bear to say more.

I considered my answer. "It's your life, your marriage, but—"

"But?"

"Henry and I agreed to stay married till Grace went to college." Not much help when her youngest was in the sixth grade. "That said, I'd have divorced him if he hadn't died."

Liz's brows lifted.

"Henry cheated. Wildly. He lied." He'd done other despicable things, but I never mentioned those. I doubted Randal Burkhart had committed Henry's sins. "Have you talked to Randal about how you feel?"

Liz nodded and her soft brown eyes glittered with tears. "He told me he was doing the best he could, and I shouldn't feel unhappy because life isn't perfect."

Randal had missed the point. By a wide mark. Liz had been honest, and his response said her unhappiness was unreasonable. "Randal's not the only man who discounts his wife's feelings."

"I know." She patted under her eyes.

"Doesn't help when it's personal." I offered her a wry, been-there-done-that smile.

"Not at all." She dropped her hands to the table's edge and stared into her coffee. "I get his point. He works incredibly hard to give the kids and me this life." Her gaze took in the club dining room, the golf course outside, and the glittering two-carat diamond on her left hand. "It's selfish to want more."

"Putting your marriage before material things isn't selfish..."

"I hear another *but* in your voice."

"We teach our sons to be competitive—baseball and football and basketball. Winners and losers. Boys grow up and replace sports' scores with dollars." Henry had. And when I earned more than he did, our marriage imploded. "Randal's doing exactly what's expected of him. He's winning. He's providing for you and the kids. He's—"

"He's never home. He travels all the time. He...I think..."

"Do you still love him?"

Now her gaze shifted to her lap. "I don't know."

Who was I to offer marital advice? "Have you considered counseling?"

"He'd never go."

"Have you asked him?"

"No," she admitted.

"It can't hurt to ask."

"Maybe." She didn't sound convinced. "Maybe I should just get over wanting more. We're comfortable. We're secure."

I didn't say a word—not one word.

"It's not as if he's cheating on me." She offered me an apologetic smile.

I leaned forward and lowered my voice. "The worst part of Henry cheating wasn't the actual infidelity; it was the women with whom he cheated. My friends. And—" my shoulders shook "—Prudence Davies."

Liz tilted her head, not understanding.

"He hurt my pride. How could he cheat on me with a woman who has horse teeth?"

Liz laughed softly.

"Ask Randal about counseling," I advised. "If Henry and I had tried counseling, I might not have become the laughing-stock of three country clubs." The gossip had been vicious.

"I will." She grimaced.

"Also, figure out what 'more' is. A job? School?" I glanced at my watch and gasped. "I hate to leave you, but I'm playing golf with my father at two."

"Oh?"

"He wants to talk about something. Pray for me."

Chapter Five

I focused on the dimpled white ball and not embarrassing myself in front of my father, who watched me from the golf cart. My grip was too tight; I loosened my hands, shook my shoulders, checked my stance, and swung.

Thwack!

The driver's face met the ball and sent it straight down the center of the fairway.

Daddy grunted his approval.

I couldn't help but smile; Daddy's approval—always hard won—still meant the world to me. I returned to the cart, dropped the driver in the bag, and climbed into the passenger seat.

Daddy shifted the cart into gear. "Nice afternoon for this."

"It is," I agreed. Mid-seventies, no humidity, a light breeze —we'd be hard-pressed to find a better day for golf.

Daddy's brow furrowed and his lips pressed into a thin line. "Your mother is upset."

We hadn't reached the putting green on the first hole and

already he'd launched into the dreaded talk—one Mother had obviously prepped him for.

"I don't find bodies on purpose."

He patted my knee. "I know, sugar."

There was a "but" lurking.

"She worries."

I stared at the fairway to the left of the cart path. The bent-grass's green was so saturated it looked painted. The weather was still cool enough for pansies to remain in ground, and their golden faces tilted toward the afternoon sun. A bank of azaleas blazed bright pink. No, the course wasn't as pretty as Augusta, but on a balmy, sun-dappled spring day it came close.

"I worry."

That shifted my gaze. Creases lined Daddy's forehead and the corners of his mouth drooped.

I reached for his hand and squeezed. I couldn't promise not to find bodies. Seemingly, they came looking for me. "I didn't know the woman who died."

"That has me worried. Why was she at your house?" He frowned. "Assuming she wasn't actually Mrs. Anarchy Jones."

"She wasn't." I was quick to reply.

"Why lie about her name?"

"I wish I knew." This discussion was getting us nowhere. "Gorgeous day."

He nodded and braked, slowing the cart to a gentle stop. "You're away."

I climbed out of the cart, grabbed an iron, and pretended the ball at my feet held all my frustrations and worries, all my parents' (especially my father's) doubts, all the responsibility for my missed trip to Italy.

Thwack!

The ball soared, then bounced onto the green.

Daddy's brows rose. "Have you been taking lessons?"

"No." I didn't smile at his backhanded praise.

With Daddy-disapproves-of-Anarchy lead weights in my stomach, I returned to the golf cart, and we drove another thirty feet to Daddy's ball.

Daddy swung his legs onto the path and his cleats rang against the hard surface. He glanced over his shoulder before stepping onto the course. "We want what's best for you, sugar."

"I appreciate that." The dryness in my voice was too pronounced—Daddy's lips compressed.

"Don't judge your mother too harshly. She wants you to be happy. We both do."

I nodded and sealed my lips. Mother wanted me to be secure, and if I was lucky happiness would follow.

"She knows what to expect from a man like Tafft. His background. His family. His friends."

I could tell him Anarchy was a California version of Hunter. The knowledge would ease his worries, and there would be a certain satisfaction in hearing Mother change her tune. Surely they could realize Anarchy was a good man without studying his family tree. "I didn't fall in love with Hunter."

Daddy looked up from his golf ball. "You're in love with Jones?"

"I am."

"How serious is this?"

"I just told you."

Daddy's mouth formed a hard line. He swung his club, sliced into a bunker, and glared at me as if his errant shot was my fault. "He's a cop."

I shrugged.

"You've already had one marriage fail because you earned more than your husband."

"That won't be an issue."

Daddy gripped his club as if he wished it were Anarchy's neck, jammed the shaft into his bag, and resumed his spot behind the golf cart's wheel. "You say that now, but when the honeymoon is over—"

"It will be my problem."

The cart didn't move.

"Before I married Henry, you told me a man's character was more important than his name or his bank balance." In retrospect, Daddy had offered me a warning I'd blithely ignored.

"I said that?"

"Ten minutes before you walked me down the aisle. You told me if I had doubts not to marry Henry."

Daddy winced. "I never liked him. He wasn't good enough for you."

"Now I've found a man with character, and you're hung up on his name and his bank balance."

Without a word, Daddy put the cart in gear and drove toward his ball.

"Don't worry about Anarchy."

His lips pursed and he patted my knee. "Worrying about my daughters is my job." He got out of the cart, pulled a wedge from his golf bag, and waded into the sand. His chip shot landed on the fairway. His narrowed eyes measured the distance to the green before he returned to the cart.

"I know what I'm doing," I told him.

"You're not thinking rationally." He dismissed the idea I might be a responsible adult and traded the wedge for an iron. "You're a woman in love."

Would a little faith be too much to ask?

Of course, if Anarchy's mother hated me, this whole discussion might be moot.

"What's wrong?" Daddy demanded.

"Wrong?"

"You winced. Something's bothering you, or maybe you're not as sure about Jones as you pretend."

I was one hundred percent certain of Anarchy and tired of Daddy's doubts. "His mother is here," I snapped. "I'm worried about meeting her."

"You're worried?"

"Yes," I admitted.

"You?" Daddy lifted a brow.

It was Anarchy's mother. If she disapproved of me the way my parents disapproved of him, family holidays would be hell. "Yes."

"Didn't someone tell me his mother was a fiber artist?"

"She is."

"That's a fancy name for someone who makes macramé plant hangers. *He* should worry. You'll meet her and realize you can do better."

There was a lot more to fiber art than plant hangers, but I wasn't about to argue that point. Not with a man who thought Henry Moore's sculptures were blobs. "You sound like Mother."

"Sometimes your mother makes a lot of sense."

"And sometimes prejudice blinds her."

Daddy grunted, strode out onto the fairway, hit the ball, and overshot the green.

I slumped in my seat. It was going to be a long afternoon.

Daddy finished plus twelve on eighteen holes. I shot four under par.

He parked the cart near the pro shop. "I'm buying drinks."

"I don't have time." He was in a black mood. The last thing I wanted to do was spend another thirty minutes with him.

"I insist. Meet me on the patio next to the grill." He disappeared into the men's locker room before I could argue.

I changed my shoes, climbed the outdoor steps to the patio, chose a table, and peeked at my watch. Five thirty. I had enough time for a quick drink with Daddy before I had to head home and get ready for dinner with Anarchy and his mother.

The patio crowd was sparse. Two men, both wearing plaid golf shorts with white belts, were deep in discussion in the shade cast by a table umbrella. They scowled at me—while women were allowed on the patio, we weren't exactly welcome.

Bill Sandhurst sat alone at a table that held a tumbler of scotch and an ashtray with his own smoking cigar. He nodded at me. "Ellison."

"Nice to see you, Bill." Blinding to see Bill. He wore lime green gingham pants, and his bald head reflected the sun's rays.

"May I get you a drink?"

As a woman, I wasn't allowed in the men's grill, and it was the closest bar.

"My father should be here any minute. How's your daughter? I heard she was sick."

Bill's face clouded. "Lucinda took her to the ER, but she's fine now."

"Gracious. I hope it wasn't serious."

"A stomach thing. Alec was always healthy." Alec was Bill's son from his first marriage. He'd been in high school when his mother passed away from cancer and in college when his father married a woman almost twenty years his junior. "And the boys have never been sick a day in their lives, but Amy—" he stared into his drink before taking an enormous sip "—the poor thing is sick all the time."

"Is it chronic? Do they know—"

"Ellison!" Daddy's voice boomed. He stood in the doorway to the grill. "Do you know what you've done?"

I cataloged my recent sins. "No."

A grin split his face. "You broke the ladies' record."

The image of a smashed turntable filled my mind, complete with a vinyl album reduced to smithereens. "What?"

"You shot four under par. You broke the club record."

A smiling waiter slipped by him with a bottle of Champagne. A second waiter carried enough glasses to serve everyone on the patio.

Bill Sandhurst clapped.

So did the gentlemen smoking cigars beneath the cover of the sunshade.

Daddy, whose chest puffed with fatherly pride, pressed a Champagne glass into my hand, then raised his own glass. "Congratulations, sugar."

"Thank you." There had to be a mistake. Any minute now the club pro would appear and tell us the club record was five under.

But he didn't.

I sipped my Champagne, listened to Daddy tell Bill about my putt to save par on the eleventh hole—*it was as if she took her game to a new level*—and wondered how quickly I could leave. At six o'clock, I shifted in my seat. "Daddy, thank you for the Champagne. I need to get home."

His face clouded. "You're sure? We should celebrate."

"I have dinner plans." My stomach completed three flips just saying the words. "We'll celebrate another night."

"What should I tell your Mother?"

I swallowed. "Tell her we talked."

He frowned. Mother expected results.

"Tell her I broke the club record."

The frown lightened.

"Tell her I'll think about everything you said." For less than a minute.

My father stood and dropped a kiss on my cheek. "I love you, sugar."

"I love you, too." I hurried to my locker, grabbed my purse, and flew home.

~

AT PRECISELY SEVEN O'CLOCK, I took a deep, centering breath, slapped a nervous smile on my face, and opened the front door.

Anarchy and his mother waited on the front stoop.

I extended my hand. "Welcome, Mrs. Jones."

Anarchy's mother was tall and thin with dark shaggy hair shot with silver. She wore glasses with lavender lenses, black pants, a black t-shirt, and a crimson batik jacket. Her hand in mine was callused and strong. "Mrs. Jones is my mother-in-law. Call me Celeste."

The tension tightening my neck eased slightly. "Welcome, Celeste."

"Thank you for having me."

"Please, come in."

Celeste paused and took in the foyer. "You have a lovely home."

"Thank you. I thought we'd sit in the living room till dinner is ready."

"What are you cooking? It smells delicious."

"I take no credit. I believe Aggie has a roast in the oven." I led Celeste into the living room and crossed to the bar cart. "What may I get you?"

"Sambuca on the rocks."

Miracle of miracles, I actually had Sambuca. I poured a healthy dose over ice and asked, "Anarchy, what will you have?"

"Scotch. Neat."

I blinked back my surprise (Anarchy seldom drank hard

liquor) and poured two fingers of Johnny Walker into an old-fashioned glass.

"Is that one of yours?" Celeste pointed to a still life hung between the front windows.

"Yes." I delivered her drink.

Anarchy took his scotch from my hands. "What are you having?"

"Wine." I returned to the bar cart and poured myself a glass.

Celeste tilted her head as if the painting was a riddle in need of solving. "Do you always paint flowers?"

I heard her unspoken criticism loud and clear. I created pretty art. "I paint a variety of subjects."

"You have talent."

"Mom." Anarchy's voice carried a warning.

"What?" Celeste smiled at her son—a sweet, innocent smile that made my blood run cold. "She's talented."

"Thank you." I ignored what she meant—I had talent and I'd sold out for commercial success—and perched on the arm of a wingback chair. "What are you working on, Celeste?" Whatever it was, it wouldn't be pretty.

"A wall piece called 'Caged Pink.'"

Anarchy screwed his eyes shut as if he were in pain.

"It explores the feminine mystique," Celeste explained.

Anarchy's eyes remained firmly closed.

"The feminine mystique?" What did that mean?

"Vaginas, dear."

My eyes widened. My cheeks warmed. What did one say to one's boyfriend's mother when she discussed vaginas? "In fiber?"

"Of course. It's a very organic piece with heavy cording representing our male oppressors."

"Fascinating." What else could I say?

Her eyes glinted behind her lavender lenses.

"Mom, let's talk about something else."

Celeste sighed and rolled her neck. "My son is embarrassed by vaginas."

Celeste and Mother could never meet. Never. Ever. Like patchouli oil and mineral water, they wouldn't mix. And Mother's head might spin off her neck.

Anarchy pressed the pads of his fingers against his left temple. "I'm not embarrassed—"

"It's my art, Anarchy. And you shouldn't be embarrassed. Vaginas are a natural and beautiful part of a woman's body."

I had one and I was embarrassed.

Anarchy drank half the scotch in his glass in one sip.

"He can't even say the word."

Anarchy covered his face with his left palm.

"You can do it, honey. It's easy: va-gi-na."

Oh. Dear. Lord.

I cast about for a new topic, but before I launched into a discussion about the weather Aggie saved me. She paused in the doorway holding a silver tray. "Rumaki?"

"Thank you!" I exclaimed. Thank you for rescuing me from the most uncomfortable conversation in recent memory. "Where are the dogs?" I stood and claimed the tray.

"Backyard." Aggie's gaze traveled from my flushed cheeks to Anarchy's still-covered face. "Dinner will be ready in twenty minutes."

"Thank you." I offered Celeste a canapé and hoped she didn't tell me she was a vegetarian.

She popped a bacon-wrapped water chestnut into her mouth. "Delicious."

"Anarchy?"

"Not now, thanks." He'd opened his eyes, and their expression said he might never be hungry again.

I put the tray on the coffee table and resumed my seat.

"So, Ellison, how did you meet my son?"

"I found a body."

"How clever of you."

"Actually, it was horrible." The memory of swimming into Madeline's cold corpse made me shudder.

"From what I hear, you find lots of bodies."

"Mom!"

"I'm unlucky that way."

"Hmph." Celeste popped another rumaki. "Where's your studio?"

"My studio?"

"I'd love to see where you paint."

"It's a mess right now."

She waved a dismissive hand. "Of course it's a mess. You're an artist."

Anarchy slumped in his seat.

The distant sound of the phone ringing made me hope for an emergency call—Libba with her keys locked in the car, Mother insisting on congratulating my golf score, the PTA demanding cookies for a bake sale. "Perhaps another time."

Celeste frowned as if unaccustomed to being denied. "Anarchy tells me you also design fabric. How talented you must be."

What had I done to this woman? "The fabric design is recent."

Celeste glanced around the living room with its conservative antiques and traditional fabrics. Her lip curled just a bit. "Have you lived here long?"

"Nearly twenty years."

"You must have been a child bride."

Henry's mother hadn't liked me. I'd been too artsy for her banker son. While she lived, she hid quick, sharp cuts in everything she said to me. Was I being too sensitive now? "I was very young." I kept my voice mild.

"Anarchy tells me your husband's been dead less than a year."

Another cut? "He died last June."

"So lovely how you've moved on."

Definitely a cut.

"Sorry to interrupt." Once again, Aggie stood in the doorway. "There's a phone call."

I stood so fast stars circled my head. "Oh?"

"His name is Chip Robertson and he said this was his only chance to chat for the next several days."

I glanced at Anarchy. "My friend in Lake Forest."

He nodded. "Take it. Mom and I will be fine."

I hurried across the foyer and paused by the study door. The police had removed their tape from the door. Aggie had cleaned up the mess they left behind. The study was immaculate. But I didn't want to enter. Instead, I turned on my heel, followed Aggie to the kitchen, and picked up the receiver. "Chip?"

"Ellison, how in the world are you?" Translation, why are you calling me?

"I'm fine. How are Sherry and the kids?"

"Never better. What can I do for you?"

"Do you know a woman named Monica Alexander?"

"I do. Why?"

Nope. Not going there. Not yet. "What can you tell me about her?"

"Sherry would be the one to ask. I know her husband better."

"Tell me about him."

"Monty went to law school because he didn't know what to do with himself, lucked into a major industrial tort, and scored big off the settlement. Something grisly in the meat-packing industry. Since then, he's invested in new companies. He's on several boards. Supports several charities. He and Monica have been married for about fifteen years. Why the questions?"

"Monica died in Henry's study."

"What? How?"

"I don't know. She gave my housekeeper a fake name. When I opened the study door she was slumped in a chair."

"Why was she at your house?"

"No idea. I never saw her before in my life."

"Was she murdered?"

"Why do you ask?"

"I heard she and Monty had a few problems."

"And?"

"And they married before Monty made his money. Pretty sure he took a dim view of dividing assets in a divorce."

"I'll pass that along."

"Still dating the detective?"

"Yes."

"Maybe that's why Monica came to see you."

"Why me? They live in Lake Forest. If she was worried about her husband killing her, wouldn't she go to the local police?"

"You two have similar backgrounds. Maybe she wanted advice."

"How did she know about me?"

Silence answered me.

"Chip?"

"About that..."

"Yes?"

"Sherry and I might have talked about you at a dinner party last weekend."

My turn for silence.

"The Alexanders said they were going to Kansas City, and your story's too good not to tell."

"How could you?"

"Sorry, Ellison. I really am. Listen, I have to get to O'Hare and catch a plane. I'll call you when I get back to Chicago. If you find out what happened to Monica, leave a message with Sherry." He hung up before I could fully express my feelings about his dining out on my misfortunes.

I returned the receiver to the cradle.

"Learn anything?" Aggie slid rolls into the oven.

"Chip thinks Monica's husband had a motive for murder."

Aggie set the timer. "How are things in the living room?"

"She hates me."

"Of course she does. You claimed her son."

"But—"

"You're an artist like she is, and you're successful."

"But—"

"You're young, beautiful, and have more style in your little finger than she does in her entire body. Also, you're smart a whip and an actual help to her son in his job."

I adored Aggie. I really did.

"Ten minutes till dinner."

"That means I have to go back in there."

Aggie offered me a wry grin. "Better you than me."

"If it sounds too awful, let Pansy in. She can break up a dinner party in seconds."

Aggie tsked. "That man is head over heels for you, and his mother will go back to California soon."

From her lips to God's ear.

Chapter Six

There were women, Mother among them, who opened their eyes in the morning ready to turn the world to their wills. Not me. I peeled open an eyelid, frowned at the sun streaming past the drapes, and wished for coffee. When no arabica-bearing genie appeared, I groaned and swung my feet to the floor.

Mr. Coffee welcomed me to the kitchen with a sunny smile.

I poured myself liquid heaven, settled onto a stool, and drank. A grateful sigh escaped my lips.

Rough night? Mr. Coffee was always solicitous.

I rubbed the back of my neck. "You have no idea." I drained then refilled my cup. "She talked about vaginas over cocktails. At dinner, she switched to male anatomy."

If Mr. Coffee had brows, they'd be at his water-line.

"I suspect it was for shock value. She wanted to scare me away." That was my theory, and I was sticking with it. I tilted my head and stared at the ceiling. Had Celeste Jones disliked me at first sight? She'd ignored every tenet of polite conversation. She'd reduced a tough police detective to a little boy who begged for his mother's silence. She'd made me wish the dining room floor would open and swallow me whole.

What did Anarchy do?

He'd taken her away as soon as she finished dessert.

Brnng, brnng.

I scowled at the phone. "I can't tell you how much I don't want to answer that."

Ignore it.

My fingers tightened around my mug, but it wasn't in me to ignore a ringing telephone. I pushed away from the counter and picked up the receiver. "Hello."

"Ellison?"

"This is she." I stared into the backyard, where the dogs policed the fence line. No cats or squirrels or rabbits dared touch their grass.

"It's Helen Winston. I'm calling to thank you for subbing at bridge yesterday."

I relaxed. "It was my pleasure."

"I felt awful cancelling, but Al is quite the perfectionist. Normally I give myself a week to prepare for a dinner party, and he sprung last night on me with only a day to prepare."

Entertaining Henry's business associates—one of the countless things I didn't miss. "How did it go?"

"One of the wives was under the weather, so I had to reset the table at the last minute. So annoying, and quite unlike her. I think she and Monty had an argument. Other than that, it went off without a hitch."

I'd had just enough coffee to latch onto that name.

"Monty?"

"Monty Alexander. His wife is Monica. Do you know them?"

I clutched the edge of the counter. "Never met them."

"Monty—short for Montague, not Montgomery—is quite

the character. So entertaining. So many droll stories. And I've never seen the man without a pink bowtie."

I stumbled toward Mr. Coffee. This was definitely a three-cup morning. Maybe four. "They're friends of yours?"

"Monty's on the board of a company Al bought in Chicago."

If I told Helen I'd found Monty Alexander's "sick" wife dead in the study, news would travel like wildfire. I pressed my palm against my mouth and searched for a response.

Helen saved me. "If they lived here, they'd fit right in."

My fingers tightened around my mug. "Where are the Alexanders staying?"

"The company booked rooms at The Alameda. Why do you ask?"

The truth led to more questions. "I've heard mixed reports about the rooms." I hadn't. Everyone who stayed there raved. "Friends are visiting this summer, and I wanted to make sure it's still up to snuff."

"Ah. Well, everyone seemed pleased. No complaints."

Clop, clop, clop.

"Helen, Grace is on her way to the kitchen. Can we talk later?"

"Of course. Thanks again for subbing." She hung up.

I returned the receiver to the cradle.

Grace burst into the kitchen wearing Baretraps, a denim skirt, and a madras plaid blouse. She scanned the counter and frowned. "No muffins?"

"Not today," I replied. My mind was at The Alameda.

"We had a whole plate yesterday." Grace's whine cut through the image of me striding into the hotel and demanding answers.

"I took some to Margaret Hamilton."

"To make up for Pansy?"

"Exactly."

She shook granola into a bowl (the shake communicated her deep disappoint in my mothering skills—I should have saved muffins for her) and poured milk. "How did your dinner go?"

I winced. "Don't ask. How was babysitting?"

She gave me a long, searching look. "Fine. They paid me three dollars an hour."

"What time did you get home?"

"Just after ten. Tell me about dinner. Do you like Anarchy's mom?"

I picked my words carefully. "Anarchy's mother is a unique individual."

"You don't like her." A lifetime spent around me and Mother let Grace translate tact into reality.

"I assure you; the feeling is mutual." As soon as Grace left for school, I'd call Anarchy and tell him about Helen's dinner party. We'd skip rehashing his mother's discussion of penis size. We'd skip the discussion of vaginas. We'd focus solely on the body in the study and why Monty Alexander lied to his hostess about his wife. "I need more coffee."

"I'll get it." Grace took the mug from my hands and refilled it, then she spooned granola and watched the dogs chase each other around the yard. "Max is so happy."

"I noticed."

"You're sure we have to send Pansy away?"

"If she doesn't get trained, we can't keep her."

Grace sighed and put her bowl in the sink.

"Dishwasher?"

I felt rather than saw her eyes roll.

Brnng, brnng.

I glared at the phone. What fresh hell was this?

Grace slammed the dishwasher door and reached for the

receiver. "Russell residence." Her head tilted. "Sure, just a minute." She extended the phone and whispered, "It's Anarchy."

Suddenly clammy fingers wrapped around the receiver. "Hello."

"You're still speaking to me?"

"It wasn't that bad." It was worse than bad. Completely awful. How-do-we-go-on terrible.

Hearing the lie, Grace huffed, waved goodbye, and slipped out the back door.

"I'm sorry about last night. Mom is passionate about her art." Which didn't begin to explain the sex-parts discussion.

"Obviously." I was sticking with my scare-Ellison-away theory. "I talked to Helen Winston this morning."

"Who?"

"She had a dinner party last night and Monty Alexander attended without his wife, Monica. He told everyone she was sick."

"Did you—"

"I didn't tell her a thing. But I did find out where he's staying."

"Ellison..." His voice was a warning, as if he expected me to grab Aggie and speed to the hotel for a quick interrogation. I wouldn't do that. Mainly because Aggie had the morning off.

"We can go together." I waited for his argument—this was police business, it was too dangerous for me, I should stick with painting.

Long seconds passed.

"I'll pick you up in thirty minutes."

I blinked, my counterarguments rendered mute. "Fine."

We hung up, and I dashed upstairs and threw on a green-and-white-print jersey dress, said a silent prayer of thanks for

Diane Von Furstenberg, pulled my hair into a French twist, and quickly did my makeup.

I was waiting at the front door when Anarchy arrived.

"You look nice." His coffee brown eyes held questions I'd never seen before.

"Thank you." He did, too.

"Where are we going?"

"The Alameda."

He frowned. "We called. They're not registered."

"The company booked and paid for the rooms. Do you think he'll be there?"

"Not if he killed his wife."

"It's official? She was murdered?" I pinched the bridge of my nose and considered returning to the kitchen for a fifth cup of coffee.

His hand closed gently around my wrist, pulling me toward the door. "She died of anaphylaxis."

"Of what?"

"An allergic reaction."

"So she wasn't murdered?"

A shadow crossed his face. "Depends on her allergies."

I hooked my handbag over my elbow and we headed to the driveway, where Anarchy opened the car door for me.

It took less than ten minutes to reach The Alameda, the Country Club Plaza's newest, nicest hotel.

The valet took Anarchy's car, and we entered the Spanish-inspired lobby.

"I'll get a room number." Anarchy strode toward the front desk.

I slipped into the lounge and gazed out the floor-to-ceiling windows. Cars whizzed by on Ward Parkway and morning joggers crowded the Plaza's sidewalks. Soon they'd be replaced by shoppers.

A man lowered his paper and glanced at me.

I stared at him. Rude—but I couldn't help myself. "Are you Monty Alexander?"

His brows rose. "Do I know you?"

"Helen Winston told me you always wear a pink bowtie."

His hand rose to his neck, where a jaunty tie rested below his chin. "You know Helen?"

I nodded and held out my hand. "I'm Ellison Russell."

His brows rose and a quizzical grin lifted his lips. "The woman who finds bodies? Chip Robertson told us about you." He rose from his chair. Monty Alexander was tall. Well over six feet. And solid. With ruddy cheeks and wild eyebrows. His hand swallowed mine. "A pleasure to meet you, Mrs. Russell."

He might not be so pleased if he knew I'd discovered his wife's body. I glanced over my shoulder and caught Anarchy's eye. What now? Did I ask Monty about his wife? "How are you enjoying Kansas City?"

"Lovely town."

"I think so. So different from Chicago. Not that Chicago isn't lovely, but it's big. And crowded. And windy." I stopped before I convinced him I was an idiot, that or swallowed my whole foot. Besides, I sensed Anarchy behind me.

"Mr. Alexander?"

"That's right," said Monty.

Anarchy held up a badge. "I'm Detective Jones."

"Detective?" Monty's eyes narrowed and his head tilted as if Anarchy and I posed a puzzle he wasn't sure he wanted to solve.

"How long has it been since you've seen your wife?"

Monty's ruddy cheeks paled, and he swayed slightly. "Monica?"

"Let's sit." Anarchy directed the unsteady man back to his chair.

I perched on a nearby settee, and Anarchy joined me.

"Has something happened to Monica?"

"How long has it been, sir?"

"We arrived on Monday, and she went to a luncheon."

"You haven't seen your wife since Monday?"

"No."

"And you didn't report her missing?"

Monty stared at his lap where his hands curled into tight fists. "We fought. There was someone else. I assumed she left me." He looked up, his face a study in apprehension. "What's happened?"

"Who was she seeing?" Anarchy cut to the most important question.

Monty adjusted his bowtie. "I don't know."

Anarchy speared Monty with a cop look—one that said lying carried serious consequences.

Monty pulled at his collar.

"She went to a luncheon?" I asked.

He nodded.

"Who was the hostess?"

"A friend from college. Lucinda Sandhurst."

I blinked. Seriously? What were the odds? Actually, in my world, not that long. My fingers itched for a telephone—one call to Lucinda and I might learn more than Monty could tell us.

"Did your wife have any allergies?" Anarchy reclaimed control of the conversation while I considered how best to ask Lucinda about her dead friend.

Monty blinked. "Allergies? Yes. She was allergic to bees."

The odds of a bee in Henry's study were exponentially longer than my knowing the woman with whom Monica ate lunch. It was too early for bees. Also, how could a bee have made its way to the study? The only time the door opened was when Aggie cleaned. Had a bee stung Monica on the front stoop? Was her death a sad accident?

Except...why had she come to my house? Why had she claimed to be Mrs. Anarchy Jones? Why had she died?

"Why are you asking these questions?" Monty's voice was suddenly raw. "What happened to Monica?"

"I'm sorry, Mr. Alexander." Anarchy's voice was gentle. "Your wife is dead."

Monty Alexander didn't react. Didn't move. Didn't blink.

"May I get you something?" I asked. "Coffee?"

His hands fisted in his lap. "There's been a mistake. Monica can't be dead. We're hosting dinner club next week."

"I'm so sorry for your loss." Trite? Absolutely. But what else could I say? "Are you sure I can't get you some coffee?"

He shook his head, refusing to believe us. Refusing coffee. "It's not possible." Monty planted his elbows on his knees and his head sank to his hands.

I glanced at Anarchy, and we exchanged a look. Was Monty Alexander the world's best actor? He had me believing in his innocence.

Almost. "You didn't tell anyone she was missing?"

Monty lifted his head and regarded me with drooping eyes. "No. She always comes back."

"This wasn't the first time she's disappeared?" Anarchy's voice carried a sharp edge.

"No. But we agreed—" he scrubbed his palms against his eyes "—no divorce while the kids are young."

"How old are your children?" I asked.

A dark cloud passed over his face. He took a deep breath and tilted his head upward. "They're seven, eight, and nine. We're good together. Divide and conquer. And we get along. We just don't—" He covered his mouth with his hand.

"You just don't love each other," I murmured.

"We care for each other. But we're not in love. We haven't been since..."

"Since?"

The cloud returned, darker this time. He rubbed a palm against his brow. "After Carrie, our youngest, was born, we ran out of energy for anything but the kids. The kids." His head lowered, and he moaned. "What will I tell them?"

There was no good answer.

I'd spent countless nights with my gaze glued to the bedroom ceiling as I worried how Grace was handling her father's death—her father's murder. I still spent time, usually from one to three in the morning, contemplating the ceiling.

For Monica and Monty Alexander's children's sake, I hoped her death was a tragic accident. Hoped but didn't believe. Not when she'd gained entry to my house using Anarchy's name.

"We'll need you to identify the body," said Anarchy.

Monty moaned again. His shoulders shuddered as if a cold wind blew through the lounge. Red rimmed his eyes, and his skin held a ghastly gray hue. The few minutes he'd spent with us had transformed him from a ruddy, confident man to a quivering husk.

My heart broke for him and his children.

"We'll find out what happened to your wife," I promised. It was a reckless promise. Three fingers of bourbon reckless. Three fingers of *tequila* reckless. And I didn't care. The three children who'd lost their mother deserved answers.

"Ellison—" Anarchy rose from the settee "—a word?"

"Of course." I stood, and he led me to the window.

"You can't promise that," he whispered.

"Too late." I'd call Lucinda—better yet, I'd stop by Lucinda's. I'd bring a gift for Amy. I'd get the lowdown on Monica Alexander.

Anarchy's lips flattened, and we both glanced at Monty, who stared at his knees. "I didn't think this through."

"Didn't think what through?"

"I need to drive him to the morgue."

The morgue? "I'll catch a cab." After I did a bit of shopping.

"Also—" Anarchy's gaze fixed on something over my left shoulder "—we need to talk."

Nothing good ever followed those words.

My heart beat in my ears. "About last night?"

His forehead creased, and he crossed his arms, but he remained fascinated by the goings-on just over my shoulder.

"I'm not the woman your mother wants for her son." There. I'd said it.

Now he looked at me. His brows lifted. "That's not true."

We both knew it was an absolute truth—like gravity, the earth rotating around the sun, no white after Labor Day. I raised a brow.

"She's different."

My mouth opened and shut.

"She'll go home. Soon. Till then—" His gaze shifted to the window.

"Till then?"

"Till then, please be patient with me. She's..."

Crazy as a June bug. "She's your mother." I had my own challenging mother. I couldn't hold Celeste against Anarchy. "I get it."

He nodded. Once. Then his gaze returned to Monty Alexander.

We'd talked, but we hadn't said anything. Did it matter that Celeste despised me? Or that I found her lacking in the sanity department? I breathed deep and reminded myself that Mother wasn't exactly an Anarchy fan.

"I'll call you later."

"Fine."

Anarchy led Monty Alexander to the valet station. I walked with them and watched as they climbed into Anarchy's car. Anarchy's gaze found mine just before he settled into the driver's seat. We stared for long seconds, our gazes filled with the things we hadn't said.

He looked away first, settled behind the wheel, and drove away.

I walked down Wornall Road to the Plaza, where I made a quick stop at Gateway for a teddy bear wrapped in the store's signature polka-dot paper. Next I popped into Bennett Schneider for a book. I surveyed the bestsellers and picked up *Spindrift*—an unexplained death might cover a sinister conspiracy. Phyliss Whitney's latest bestseller would make a nice gift for Lucinda.

I paid for the book, asked the clerk to call me a cab, and browsed while I waited. Even as I flipped through the latest issues of *Vogue* (my fragrance horoscope), *Cosmo* (overcome my fears), and *Town & Country* (lively lipsticks and the fine art of kissing), I thought about my promise to Monty Alexander.

Hopefully Lucinda knew something.

Chapter Seven

Lucinda Sandhurst opened her front door wearing a new Lilly Pulitzer shift. I recognized the pattern—blue and white pandas gamboling amongst Kelly green vines—from the spring collection. A cardigan sweater that matched the pandas draped over her shoulders. She smiled politely. "Ellison, what a lovely surprise." *Why are you here without calling first?*

"Bill told me Amy was sick." I held up the wrapped teddy bear and the Bennett Schneider bag. "And a little something for you."

"How kind of you. Please—" she opened the door wider "—come in."

Lucinda and Bill lived in an enormous Colonial. Pecan paneling covered the foyer walls. That paneling was the only thing Lucinda didn't change when she married Bill and moved into his house. She'd opted for a style considerably more modern than the first Mrs. Sandhurst.

"May I offer you coffee?"

"I'd love that." I followed her to a space-age kitchen. White cabinets without any visible handles, sleek white countertops, white appliances (someone had even covered Mr. Coffee's yellow gingham with white contact paper), a glass table, clear plastic chairs, and an orange ceiling.

"Sit." She waved at the table and poured coffee into two white mugs. "Do you take cream or sugar?"

"Cream if you have it."

She put the mugs on the table, poured cream into a small pitcher, then joined me. "I hear a celebration is in order."

I blinked.

"Bill told me you broke the club record."

Oh. That. "I suppose I did."

"I bet Piper Osborne is spitting nails." Piper had held the club record for years—a fact she seldom failed to mention. "If I were you, I'd watch my back."

"I had a lucky day." I ignored the warning and sipped my coffee. "How's Amy?"

"Poor baby. I got her to the hospital just in time."

"What's wrong?"

"The doctors are completely baffled."

If they didn't know the illness, they couldn't prescribe a cure. "How awful."

She nodded and her eyes filled with tears. "It is. Bill and the doctors say it's a good thing I keep such an eye on her. I saved her life by taking her to the emergency room."

"I can't imagine." Grace had suffered through chicken pox, the occasional bout with strep throat, stomach flu (three times), and more head colds than I cared to count, but she'd never been seriously ill. I took a bracing sip of coffee. "Please let me know if there's anything I can do."

Lucinda's bottom lip trembled. "That's so kind. Thank you."

"I mean it."

She hid the quaver in her chin with her palm, and I quickly

changed the subject. "Did you hear I found another body?" More coffee. This conversation called for more coffee. I downed a large sip. "In my late husband's study."

"How terrible."

"The woman who died—her name was Monica Alexander."

Lucinda's jaw dropped. "Monica?"

"Yes."

"Dead?"

My brain would not—absolutely not—conjure the image of Monica slumped in the club chair...Oops. I scraped my hair away from my face. "I'm afraid so."

Shock slackened Lucinda's face. "What happened?"

"A bee sting. She was allergic."

"That can't be. I saw her just the other day. I invited a group for lunch. Monica's chums here in Kansas City. If I'd known the two of you were friends, I would have included you."

"We weren't."

Lucinda's face clouded with confusion.

"I never met her."

Lucinda adjusted the sweater hanging on her shoulders. "Why was she at your house?"

"Mom?"

Both our heads swiveled.

Amy Sandhurst was thin and pale, with lavender crescents smudged beneath her hazel eyes. She wore a pink lawn night-gown, and her blonde hair hung limp around her shoulders.

"You're out of bed," her mother scolded.

"I'm hungry."

"I'll fix you something." Lucinda nodded toward the cheer-fully wrapped box. "Say hello to Mrs. Russell. She brought you a gift."

Amy shifted her gaze from the gift to me. "Thank you, Mrs. Russell."

"Go ahead," said her mother. "Open it."

"She's hungry." Surely that was a good sign. "I'll get out of your hair so you can feed her. When Grace is sick, a returned appetite is a good sign."

Lucinda went to the refrigerator and opened the door. "Do you want some Jell-O?"

"Yes, please. And some crackers?" Amy climbed onto a kitchen chair.

"I'll get going."

"Please stay. We haven't opened our gifts." She spooned lime Jell-O into a cereal bowl, put the bowl on a plate, and added a handful of Saltines.

Amy grabbed a spoon and inhaled the Jell-O faster than I downed my first-of-the-morning coffee. The bowl was empty in seconds. The child was definitely on the mend.

"Remind me what grade you're in."

Amy looked up from scraping her bowl. "Third."

"Do you like school?"

She nodded and nibbled the corner off a cracker.

"What's your favorite subject?"

"Art."

"Really? I have an art studio. When you're feeling better, would you like to come paint at my house?"

Amy cast a hopeful look at her mother.

"We don't want to bother you." Lucinda frowned at her daughter. "Mrs. Russell is a famous artist. She doesn't need children in her studio."

"I'd love her to visit. I wouldn't offer if I didn't mean it."

"Can I, Mommy? Please?"

"When you're feeling better."

A mutinous expression glided across Amy's face and her narrow shoulders squared. "I am feeling better."

"Young lady, you just got out of the hospital."

"I'm better." The stubborn tilt of Amy's chin reminded me of her father. She bit into the last cracker as if it was responsible for thwarting her plans.

"We'll plan a visit soon." I handed her the box from Gateway. "In the meantime, why don't you open this?"

She ripped through the paper, opened the lid, and gasped. "He's so cute!" She wrapped her arms around the bear, and the box fell from her lap to the floor. "Thank you, Mrs. Russell."

"You're welcome. That bear needs a name."

"Oliver. His name is Oliver." She sat Oliver on her lap and stroked his soft fur. "He's the best bear ever."

"I'm glad you like him."

She smiled at me. "I love him."

Lucinda collected the dropped box and the shredded wrapping paper. "Amy, take Oliver upstairs and go back to bed. You need your rest, and I need to talk to Mrs. Russell."

Hugging the bear tight to her chest, Amy slipped off her chair, and gave me a final shy smile. "Thank you."

"We'll paint soon," I promised.

She nodded and disappeared up the back stairs.

"You must be so relieved."

"She's still fragile." Lucinda put the box and the wadded-up paper on the counter. "More coffee?"

"I should go."

"Wait. I haven't opened my gift." She slid the book from the bag and eyed the cover. "This looks marvelous. Thank you."

"You're welcome. Taking care of children can mean we don't take time for ourselves. I hope you enjoy it."

"I'm sure I will." She flipped through the pages. "About Monica..."

"Yes?"

"You didn't talk to her?"

"No." Now was my chance. "Who else was at the luncheon?"

Lucinda looked up from the open book. "A handful of girls who went to Sweet Briar. Me, Jinx, Liz Spencer, and Caroline Peters. My peonies are blooming, and I used the pink ones for the table arrangement."

"You had the luncheon here?" I'd assumed she'd hosted at the club.

"I used that new caterer everyone's been talking about. Mac something or other. He did a wonderful spring salad and shrimp scampi."

"Sounds delicious." Mac was Aggie's new beau, and I had introduced him to the world of catering ladies' luncheons. He might have noticed something. And if he didn't, Jinx was a dear friend and an avid information collector. I'd call them both as soon as I got home. "I'll let you get back to your morning."

She held up the book. "Thank you for thinking of us."

"You're most welcome. And I meant what I said—I'd love for Amy to visit my studio."

"I'll call you when she's feeling better.".

THE FOYER SEEMED dark for such a sunny day, as if ill-fated clouds gathered above my house. "Aggie," I called.

She appeared in the kitchen door, wiped her hands on a tea towel embroidered with mushrooms, and scowled at the chandelier.

"Has anything happened?" A surprise visit from Mother, a surprise visit from Anarchy's mother, a second body?

"No. Why?"

Should I tell her about the bad vibes?

Her scowl deepened. "Two bulbs out. I may need to run to the hardware store."

I looked up. Sure enough, there was a good reason for the dim entry. I breathed a silent, relieved sigh. "How was your morning off?"

She touched her hair. "I visited the salon."

"Your hair looks great." I loved Aggie's corkscrew curls (easy to love when I didn't have to handle humidity, frizz, or hair that had a mind of its own). The salon had successfully tamed the wildness—for at least a day. "Date night?"

She nodded and a dreamy smile curled her lips.

"Mac catered a luncheon at Lucinda Sandhurst's earlier this week."

Aggie stood straighter—as if she sensed the shoe about to drop.

"Monica Alexander was there."

Her eyes widened and she dropped the tea towel.

"I'm wondering if Mac noticed anything."

"He doesn't always see the guests. He cooks and hires a waiter to serve."

"It can't hurt to ask."

"He's picking me up at six." She bent and retrieved the tea towel. "There are a few phone messages for you."

"From whom?"

"Libba, your mother, and someone named Piper." The dogs sidled past her, clicked their nails on the hardwood floors, and looked up at me expectantly. They'd like a walk, please. Now, please.

I scratched behind Pansy's ears. "Remind me what time the trainer arrives."

"Two o'clock." Aggie glanced at her watch as if the moments till pickup dragged. "Have you had lunch?"

"No."

"There's quiche, roast beef for sandwiches, or chef salad."

"Salad, please."

She nodded and returned to the kitchen in a swirl of turquoise kaftan.

Surprisingly, the dogs followed me to my bedroom, where I traded the dress for khaki slacks, a V-neck sweater, and navy kilties with white piping.

Pansy nudged me, and I stroked her head. "Time for you to learn some manners, missy."

She regarded me with liquid eyes—eyes that promised perfect obedience.

I wasn't fooled. "Three weeks will fly by."

Max's stubby tail and Pansy's feathered one wagged in unison.

"Do you want to go too?" If Max pined for Pansy, the three weeks she spent with the trainer would feel endless.

He grinned a response.

"What does that mean? Trainer or no trainer?"

Brnng, brnng.

I circled the bed and picked up the receiver. "Hello."

"You're home," Libba accused.

"I've been here less than five minutes."

"May I come over?"

Now? "Of course. Is something wrong?"

"Jimmy."

"Still?"

"I'll tell you when I get there." She hung up.

The dogs and I headed for the kitchen, where Aggie had tossed Romaine lettuce, cherry tomatoes, hard-boiled eggs, bits of grilled chicken, and grated cheddar in a pasta bowl.

"This looks delicious. Thank you."

"My pleasure."

I settled on a stool, picked up a fork, and smoothed a napkin over my lap. "Libba's on her way over."

"Has she eaten lunch?"

"I didn't ask." I drizzled Aggie's homemade dressing on the salad, took a bite, and moaned. Salads didn't usually elicit moans, but Aggie was an exceptional cook.

She watched me eat and wiped down the perfectly clean counter. "I've been thinking..."

I paused with the second bite halfway to my mouth. "About?"

"The woman who died."

"What about her?" I couldn't help but see her slumped in Henry's office. "Anarchy told me she had an allergic reaction to a bee sting."

"A bee sting?" Aggie's brows met over her nose. "We don't have bees."

"I know. Did one sting her on her way here? How long between a sting and the reaction?" I glanced at my loaded fork; we'd fallen into a rabbit hole. "What were you thinking?"

"The dead woman wanted to tell you something."

I nodded. And chewed. And came close to moaning again.

"Something salacious," she suggested.

I raised a brow.

"Or dangerous," she continued. "Something she wanted someone else to handle."

"Like a hot potato?" When Grace was little, mothers organized games of hot potato at birthday parties. The children passed around a potato, and when the music stopped the child holding the potato was out.

"Exactly!" Aggie grinned at the analogy. "She wanted to pass you a hot potato and she used Anarchy's name so you'd see her."

"And since I didn't know her real name, I couldn't pass it back. But why me?" An almost existential question.

Aggie wadded up the paper towel with which she'd attacked the counters. "You have a reputation for solving crimes."

Wrong. "I have a reputation for finding bodies."

"And catching killers."

"She wanted to tell me about a murder?" That couldn't be right. Monica's was the only recent death. Touch wood.

Aggie nodded so hard her dangly earrings bobbed. "Or she came to warn you."

That gave me pause. Had Monica Alexander learned something dangerous? If so, how? I needed to talk to Jinx.

Ding, dong.

"You eat," Aggie instructed. "I'll get the door."

I forked another bite of salad.

"He says I'm ashamed of him." Libba stood in the kitchen doorway with her hands on her hips and her eyes set to laser.

"Are you?"

"No," she snapped. Her laser vision burned a hole through my forehead. "Why is it okay for a man in his sixties to be with a woman in her thirties, but I can't date a man who's eight years younger?"

I held up my hands in surrender. "I never said you shouldn't date him."

"But you thought it."

"What do you need, Libba?"

"I need an invitation to cocktails. Tonight."

"Done. Aggie has plans so I can't invite you to dinner. Not unless you want him poisoned." My cooking wasn't the best.

"Drinks at five thirty, then we'll go out for dinner. You can come with us. Is Anarchy free?"

"His mother came for a visit."

"His mother? Why didn't you tell me? Do you like her? Does she like you?"

I scrunched my face.

"What happened?" She sat on the stool next to mine, reached into my salad, extracted a cherry tomato, and popped into her mouth.

I recounted Celeste's discussion of vaginas.

"She sounds like a pistol."

I moaned—and not a this-salad-is-amazing moan.

"Any woman who can discuss vaginas with her son's girl-friend has balls."

"Or she wants the girlfriend to run for the hills."

"Good point. But she doesn't know you. You're not the running type."

I slapped her hand away from cadging another tomato. "Aggie can make you one."

"I'm not hungry." An evil grin settled on her lips. "Will you introduce her to Frances?"

"Are you kidding? They can never, ever meet."

"It would make for an interesting evening."

"It would make for World War Three."

Libba's grin widened. "Better than a soap opera."

"Spoken like someone who does not want to bring her beau to cocktails."

Libba wrinkled her nose and stuck out her tongue. "What are you doing this afternoon?"

"The trainer is picking up Pansy. When she's gone, I'll paint." And call Jinx. And write a list of questions for Mac.

"I hoped we could shop."

"I don't need anything."

"When has that ever stopped you? Especially after you've found a body."

"What do you mean?"

She swiped another tomato. "Retail therapy."

"Don't be ridiculous."

My best friend tilted her head and smirked.

I measured out a tiny distance between my thumb and pointer finger. "You might have a point. A small one. But you're in no position to judge."

"Who's judging? Just pointing out the obvious." She eyed my tomato-less salad. "So, Swanson's?"

"Not today." I had an investigation to meddle in.

Chapter Eight

Grace stood in my bedroom doorway and eyed the navy slacks and silk shirt I wore. "Are you going out?"

"Libba's bringing Jimmy for cocktails. When they leave, I'm collapsing on the couch, eating leftover quiche, and watching *The Rockford Files*. You're going to a concert?"

"The Eagles. What about Max?" The dog, who'd curled up at the foot of my bed (I didn't have the heart to kick him off), lifted his head and sighed. "He seems depressed."

"He does." Max's long sighs and doleful stares had kept me company since the trainer left with Pansy. "I'll take him out after *Rockford*."

Max reacted with a single wag of his stubby tail.

"She's coming back. Soon."

He gazed at me with mournful, puppy-dog, my-heart-is-breaking eyes.

"Promise."

He settled his chin on his paws and huffed.

"Is Anarchy coming over?"

"No. His mother is still in town." The acid in my voice

surprised me. Celeste was a challenge, but she was still Anarchy's mom. And it wasn't as if Mother made Anarchy feel liked.

I glanced at the clock on the bedside table and walked toward the door. "They'll be here in a minute and I need to check the flowers." I loved lilies but hated when pollen from the anthers discolored the petals.

Grace frowned. "Are you serving hors d'oeuvres?"

"Aggie made a cheese ball and crackers. Also, there are stuffed mushrooms ready. If Libba's late—" which was likely "—all I have to do is put them in the oven."

Grace lifted her left brow. Could I be trusted to set a timer, hear the timer, and not set the kitchen on fire? Her pursed lips said I couldn't.

"Ye of little faith."

Now she grinned. "You're not exactly a cook."

"Mac's not picking Aggie up till six. If Libba's close to on time, she'll bake them."

Grace held up her hand and crossed her fingers.

A couple of minor conflagrations and your daughter never let you forget them.

Ding, dong.

Libba? Early? The kitchen was safe from my cooking attempts.

Max lifted his head, his eyes suddenly filled with hope.

"It's Libba and Jimmy." Early. In hell, the demons threw snowballs.

He sighed as if I'd broken his doggy heart. Again.

I took one last glance in the mirror and headed downstairs.

Aggie, resplendent in a kaftan that tottered between mint and turquoise, stood at the open front door. The stiff set of her shoulders sounded alarm bells in my brain.

"Aggie?"

She stepped aside.

Celeste Jones stood on my front stoop.

Oh. Dear. Lord.

Celeste spotted me and smiled. "Ellison, Anarchy's working. I thought we should spend more time together—get better acquainted." Her smile didn't reach her eyes.

I couldn't form words. Not even one.

With Mother-like determination, Celeste brushed past an equally mute Aggie. "Just a quick chat. There are things that must be said."

No. There weren't. "I'm sorry, Celeste." Not sorry. "I'm expecting guests."

"I won't stay long."

This was Anarchy's mother. And he'd been unfailingly polite to mine. Short of physically kicking her out, I was stuck. I swallowed a coffee-mug-sized ball of dread and forced a smile. "Shall we sit?"

Celeste followed me into the living room.

I crossed to the bar cart. "What may I get you?"

"Your maid doesn't serve drinks?"

Annoyance tightened each vertebra in my spine. "She's my housekeeper, not my maid. And no, she doesn't."

Celeste plonked onto the settee. "Wine."

"White or red?"

"Red."

She watched as I opened a bottle and poured.

I handed her a glass and settled onto a wingback chair.

Celeste took a small sip, wrinkled her nose, and regarded me with narrowed eyes.

I pretended her gaze didn't feel like sandpaper on my skin.

"My son likes you." She wrinkled her nose as if she'd smelled sewer gas. "You're wrong for him." She waved a hand at my living room. "This is wrong for him."

I wasn't wrong for Anarchy, and Celeste should butt out. "This?" My voice was mild. Amazing, since inside I was seething.

"I raised my son to value people over things."

"That's how most people raise their children."

Celeste's lips thinned and her gaze catalogued the living room's antiques, the Lalique ashtrays, the Revolutionary-era silver candlesticks on the mantle, the Chinese porcelain, and the Oriental beneath our feet. "This is the world I left behind."

"Your objection to me is that I have too much money?"

"And too many of the attitudes that go with it."

"What are those?"

"Your life is shallow."

I clenched my hands in my lap. "You don't know anything about my life."

"Golf, tennis, bridge, committee meetings, book club, I can go on..."

Heat flushed my cheeks. The grain of truth in Celeste's words was just that—a grain. I did those things, but my life was so much more. "My daughter, my art, your son."

Her eyes narrowed as if I'd thrown a gauntlet. "You'd walk away from all this?"

"Why would I do that?"

"Anarchy deserves better—deserves more than Friday night cocktails at the club and vacations on Martha's Vineyard." Again with the grain of truth.

Raised by a Sherman tank who rolled over the smallest sign of independence, arguing with an older woman didn't come naturally to me. But this was an argument worth having. "Your son deserves a woman who loves him."

"And that's you?" Her voice was a sneer.

"It is." I hid the sudden tremor in my hands by clasping

them together. "I'll be sure and tell him you stopped by." I stood, code for *get the hell out of my house.*

Celeste didn't budge. "Stay away from my son."

Oh. Dear. Lord.

Ding, dong.

The murmur of voices was followed by Libba and Jimmy's appearance in the doorway.

"You're here." I hurried to them and gave Libba a quick, grateful hug. "Jimmy—" I kissed his cheek "—how nice to see you."

A smile lifted his boyish cheeks, and his eyes sparkled. "Good to see you, Ellison."

"I can't believe we haven't done this sooner. Please, come in. What may I get you?" I glanced at Celeste, who stared at my friends with poorly disguised disdain. "Libba, Jimmy, this is Celeste Jones."

Libba's eyes narrowed as she took in the woman on the couch. Long graying hair held back from her face with a stick and piece of leather, a linen smock, loose pants. Celeste dressed like an artist.

"Celeste, meet Libba and Jimmy." For the life of me, I couldn't remember Jimmy's last name, so I omitted Libba's as well.

Celeste studied my friends—Libba's satin jumpsuit with a deep cleavage-revealing vee, Jimmy's khaki pants and the navy blazer that struggled to contain his biceps. Her upper lip curled in a sneer that would do Mother proud.

"It's a pleasure to meet you, Celeste," said Libba.

Woof!

We all looked at Max, but Jimmy crouched and rubbed my lonely dog's shoulders.

"You've made a friend for life. What may I get you to drink?"

"Martini." Libba's request wasn't a surprise. The ingredients waited on the bar cart.

"A beer?"

"Libba, if you'll mix your own drink, I'll run to the kitchen for a beer. I'll be back in two shakes." It was a coward's escape, but I didn't care. I needed a moment away from the gorgon in the living room.

When I entered the kitchen, Aggie looked up from sliding a tray of mushroom caps into the oven. I pressed my palms against my flaming cheeks. "Do we have any beer?"

"There's a six-pack of Budweiser in the spare fridge. I'll get it."

"Thank you." I leaned over the kitchen island and took a deep breath. Celeste Jones had flat out told me I was wrong for her son—too materialistic, not good enough. Mother, at her worst, would never tell Anarchy he wasn't good enough for me. She might think it. She might tell me. But she'd never say it to him.

I drew air into my belly, held it till the shaking in my hands eased, and exhaled slowly.

Aggie reappeared with an empty Pilsner glass and a can of cold beer on a silver tray. "Are you okay?"

"Fine," I lied.

I took the tray from her hands and walked into the front hall just in time to see the front door swing open.

Mother looked at me, the tray, the beer. "Who's here?"

"Libba and her beau."

Mother wrinkled her nose. "The fireman?"

"Yes." How could I get rid of her?

Daddy appeared behind her holding a bottle of Moet Chandon like a trophy. "Hey, sugar, we came to toast your record."

If there was a single accomplishment less likely to impress Anarchy's mother, I couldn't think of it.

Daddy stepped into the foyer and closed the door.

There was no escaping the next few minutes.

My face felt brittle. My lips felt numb. But I led my parents into the living room, served Jimmy his beer, and said, "Mother, Daddy, I'd like to introduce you to Celeste Jones. Celeste, my parents, Frances and Harrington Walford."

"Jones?" Mother's tone could freeze the Pacific. Solid.

"This is Anarchy's mother."

Daddy stepped forward and offered his hand. "Pleased to meet you, Celeste."

"Likewise." If Mother's tone was cold enough to make it snow in Hawaii, Celeste's could form icebergs off the Florida coast.

With the image of enormous ice cubes cooling Miami Beach, I searched for something to say.

Libba saved me. "Frances, Harrington, how lovely to see you. You remember Jimmy?"

I wasn't sure my father had ever met Jimmy, but both my parents nodded.

"You saved the cat," said Mother.

Jimmy grinned. "That's me."

"You're a fireman?" Celeste's brows touched her hairline.

"Yes, ma'am."

"And you're with her?"

Jimmy tore his adoring gaze away from Libba and frowned.

"You're young, you're virile, you're handsome, and she's—"

"She's a smart, funny, beautiful woman with a heart of gold," I finished. If Celeste talked about younger, tighter vaginas, Mother would expire.

"We're happy, and age is just a number." Jimmy reached for Libba's hand, and his shrug dismissed Celeste's implied insults.

Daddy, who'd survived forty-five years with Mother, took the room's temperature and tried to deflect. He held up the Champagne. "We're celebrating, Celeste. I hope you'll join us."

"Celebrating?"

"Ellison broke the ladies' club record." He beamed at me.

"You're a golfer?" Celeste's voice was sweet, but her smirk was pure vinegar.

"Not really. I had a lucky day."

"Now, sugar, you know you're good." Daddy presented Celeste a flute filled with sparkling wine. "She'd be great if she played more, but she's dedicated to her art."

"Is she?"

Daddy served Libba, then looked back at Celeste. "The only thing more important to her is taking care of Grace."

Mother held her flute with stiff fingers and shot me a look. "When did you arrive in Kansas City, Celeste? Ellison didn't tell me you were here."

I very nearly rolled my eyes. If Mother had known, it wasn't as if she'd have invited Celeste to the club for lunch.

Not that country-club-hating Celeste would defile the soles of her Birkenstocks on the club's rarified carpets.

They had only one thing in common. I crossed my fingers they didn't discover the one thing about which they agreed— neither wanted Anarchy and me together.

Daddy raised his glass. "To Ellison and the best round of golf I've ever seen."

I MELTED into the family room couch. My fingers clutched a wine glass. My gaze followed James Garner across the screen. He'd teamed with Stephanie Powers to track down a murderer in a case the police dismissed as an accident.

Max lay curled next to me with his head in my lap.

Aside from stroking his ears, I might never move again.

I'd had bad nights. Nights I found bodies. Nights I worried myself sick over Grace. One memorable night I'd run over my husband. But tonight ranked as the worst.

Celeste hated me. And Mother and Daddy. And Libba. Jimmy, she liked.

Brnng, brngg.

I ignored the phone.

Brnng, brngg.

Max growled.

"I'm done," I told him. "There is no way I'm getting up to answer a phone."

Brnng, brngg.

"The machine will get it. Have you noticed that Rockford and Anarchy dress alike?"

Max huffed.

I rested my head on the couch back and stared at the ceiling.

Max nudged my hand for more pets.

On the screen, Rockford saved Stephanie Powers' character and caught the killer.

On the couch, Max nudged me again.

"You want a walk?"

Max lifted his head.

"Fine." I stood, swayed, and found my balance.

Max yawned, lowered his front paws to the floor, and walked them forward till his body stretched long. Only then did he allow his back paws to touch the carpet.

Brnng, brngg.

Again? I scowled at the phone.

Brnng, brngg.

I strode to the desk and jerked the receiver off the cradle. "Hello." A bark, not a greeting.

"Ellison, it's Lucinda. Did I catch you at a bad time?"

Yes! "Actually, I'm on my way out the door with the dog." Almost true. "May I call you later?"

"I just called to thank you again for thinking of Amy and me."

"It was my pleasure."

"So thoughtful of you—"

Woof!

"Is that your dog? I'll let you get to your walk. Talk soon." She hung up, and I wished all my conversations were that brief.

I'd have to call and apologize for my curtness. Tomorrow. Maybe the day after.

I hooked the leash on Max's collar, and we slipped outside into the warm night.

The air was soft and flower-scented—and I couldn't help but think where I'd be if Monica Alexander hadn't died in my study. I'd be breathing warm flower-scented air in Italy. No Celeste. No Mother. No one but Anarchy and me.

Max stopped and sniffed a fire hydrant.

I waited, staring at the sky's deepening lavender. The streetlights cast golden halos. Beyond their glow, a handful of stars glimmered. The manicured lawns looked like black velvet, and the house's lit windows hinted at happy families. This neighborhood was home. I'd learned to ride a bike on its sidewalks, had my first kiss behind the Tremaines' lilac bush, learned to drive on its wide streets, and covered every inch of pavement when Grace had colic and only walks in her stroller quelled her cries. Celeste could turn up her nose at my home, but Anarchy seemed to like it, and I wasn't leaving.

Max trotted forward, pulling me in his wake. He looked over his shoulder and sighed. The night's diversions were a pale reflection of what they could be if only I hadn't sent Pansy away.

"I'm not a villain."

He huffed.

"She'll be back before you know it."

Max eyed a rabbit but couldn't find the enthusiasm for a chase.

We stopped at the corner and watched a dark sedan glide by.

"Which way?"

Max pulled right. The Sunset route (named for a street, not the sky).

"Are you sure? No sidewalks."

He pulled harder, and I relented.

Peonies and lilacs scented the air, and the tension in my neck eased. Slightly.

I tightened my hold on the leash and stepped onto the curb as a station wagon passed us.

My mind returned to the living room where Mother and Celeste had stared each other down. Celeste had taken a tiny sip of Champagne, put her glass on the coffee table, and said, "I'm leaving. Think about what I said. You and Anarchy aren't right for each other." Her lip had curled. "This isn't right for him."

Daddy had seen her to the door.

"What a sensible woman," said Mother.

"She thinks Anarchy's too good for me."

Mother's brows lifted and her lips pinched.

"I'm too shallow." I talked around the tightening in my throat.

"That's ridiculous," said Libba.

"Preposterous." Mother was scandalized. "If anything, you're too good for him."

"Stop." I'd held up my hands to dam the flow of words and turned to Jimmy. "I apologize. There are nights with no drama. I hope you'll come again and let me prove it."

"I'd like that." He'd polished off his beer. "Libba, we should get going."

"We should?" She glanced at Mother. "Right. We should."

They left me.

Mother looked as if a lecture poised on the tip of her tongue, but Daddy led her to the car—they didn't want to be late for a party at the Larsons'.

I'd stumbled to the kitchen, cut myself a slice of cold quiche, refilled my wine glass, and collapsed in front of the television.

Max tugged on the leash and reclaimed my attention.

A car passed us, and I blinked in the headlights' glare.

"Shall we head home?"

Max stopped and lifted his nose, sniffing the spring air. Headlights glinted on his silver fur, and I stepped onto the curb. A car was coming up behind us.

The too-loud roar of the approaching engine was my only warning.

A fender slammed into me, and I flew.

I lost my grip on Max's leash.

He yelped.

I tumbled across the car's hood.

I saw taillights.

Then I saw black.

Chapter Nine

Beep.

My shoulder ached.

Beep.

My head ached.

Beep.

My toes ached.

Beep.

And what was that beeping? I pried open an eye and recognized the raw-oatmeal-colored walls of the hospital. The beeping came from a machine attached to my arm.

My fingers scrabbled for a call button. How long had I been here? The sun brightened the window. Morning? Where was Max? Was he hurt? I found the button and jabbed. And jabbed.

A smiling nurse entered the room. "You're awake."

That much was obvious. "What happened?"

"You were hit by a car."

The headlights, the hood, the collision with the pavement came back to me. "What happened to Max?"

"Max?"

"My dog."

Her brows drew together. "I don't know."

"Is Mother here? Grace?" Anarchy?

"Your family went to the coffee shop. I'm sure they'll be back soon."

"How badly am I hurt?"

"You'll make a full recovery."

Good to know, but not what I asked.

"Ellison?" Anarchy stood in the doorway. Wrinkles creased his forehead and his skin was uncharacteristically pale. "Grace called me. I got here as soon as I could."

My eyes filled with tears.

Anarchy pushed past the nurse, sat on the edge of the bed, and took my hand. "Where are you hurt? What's wrong?"

It wasn't pain that wet my lashes. After nearly twenty years married to Henry, being with someone who actually cared took getting used to—and made me weepy. I forced a smile. "I'm fine. Or I will be. I've been promised a full recovery."

"Doctor Abbott will be here soon." The nurse stared at Anarchy as if she'd never seen a handsome man before. "May I get you anything?"

"Coffee," I snapped. "Please."

She nodded and disappeared into the hallway.

Anarchy's fingers brushed my cheek, and I leaned into their warmth.

"What happened?"

"I was walking Max—what happened to Max?"

"According to Grace, Max is fine."

I relaxed into my pillows. "Thank heavens. Who hit me?"

Anarchy's lips thinned.

"They didn't stop?"

"Apparently, Max sat next to you and barked till someone

came to investigate. Did you see the car?" The expression in his eyes was dangerous.

I pictured the dark street. "I was on the curb." My next thought chilled me, and I shivered beneath the hospital's light blanket. "They hit me on purpose."

"You're sure?" A jeweler could cut diamonds on the edge in Anarchy's voice.

"I was halfway onto the Stanleys' lawn. There were no cars parked on the street, both lanes were clear. Whoever hit me was drunk or did it on purpose."

Anarchy's hold on my hand tightened.

"Why?" I asked. "Why me?" It was as if the universe conspired against me.

With his free hand, Anarchy rubbed his chin. "You found a body."

"True. But I didn't know Monica and I don't know anything about her death." A horrible thought flashed through my brain. "Could she have come to my house to warn me?"

"About what?"

Frustration and my headache made thinking a challenge. "I don't know. Has anyone checked Prudence's car for dents?" Prudence might not scheme my death, but if an opportunity to put me six feet under arose, she'd take it.

"I'll send someone by." He brushed a strand of hair from my face and stared into my eyes. "I'll keep you safe. I promise."

I was so tired of people trying to kill me. "Maybe it was an accident." It wasn't, but denial was cozy and warm compared to stark reality.

"I'm not taking risks. Not with your safety. I'm moving into your spare bedroom."

My heart skipped a beat.

Beep, beep, beep.

Dratted machine. I lifted my head off the pillow. "You can't move in; your mother is visiting."

"She wasn't invited to Kansas City. I told her to go home."

"She came to see me last night."

He stiffened. "Oh?"

"She doesn't approve of me."

"I imagine not."

Ouch.

"Mom wouldn't approve if you were a barefoot art-for-art's-sake beatnik who lived in a barn. There's no winning her approval. Don't try."

"She loves you."

"And I love her, but there's a lot of baggage. Hers and mine." He glanced out the window and a scowl darkened his face. He was digging through those bags and didn't like what he found. But when his gaze returned to me, a smile touched his lips. He leaned forward and those smiling lips brushed against mine.

Beep, beep, beep.

"Ellison Walford Russell!"

Yikes! My heart careened as if I were a teenager who'd been caught kissing on her parents' couch. Then I glared. At Mother.

She had the worst timing ever.

Grace grinned. "You're awake!"

Anarchy straightened—slowly—and kept his hold on my hand. "Good morning, Frances. Hey, Grace."

Now that he wasn't kissing me, Mother ignored him. "You dislocated your shoulder."

That explained the shoulder ache.

"You have a mild concussion."

That explained the headache.

"You're lucky to be alive."

She didn't have an explanation for my aching toes?

"And you're kissing?"

She knew the answer to that question.

"They already fixed your shoulder." Grace sat opposite Anarchy and claimed my free hand. "I'm so glad you're okay."

"How's Max?"

"Fine. I told him he's a hero."

"Don't. It'll go to his head." I squeezed her hand.

She squeezed back. "Too late."

A man (wire-rimmed glasses, a stethoscope draped round his neck, and a crisp white coat) pushed into the already crowded room.

"Good morning, Doctor—" Mother squinted at the name embroidered on his coat "—Abbot. I'm Frances Walford, and this is my daughter, Ellison Russell." Mother was the hospital's board chairman and her introduction served as a blunt hint. *Take care of my daughter.*

"A pleasure to meet you, Mrs. Walford." His pale blue eyes were enormous behind his glasses. "How's our patient?"

"My shoulder aches."

"It'll do that for the next few days."

"May I go home?"

He glanced at Mother, and his Adam's apple bobbed. "You hit your head. We'd like to keep an eye on you for a day or two."

"One day." My headache wasn't anything a few aspirin couldn't handle. "No more."

Dr. Abbott nodded, noted something on a chart at the foot of my bed, and made his escape.

"I'll get Mom on a plane." Anarchy's eyes held a silent apology for whatever she'd said to me last night.

Mother turned to him. "I met your mother."

His eyes widened in horror.

I winced and nodded. Yes, it had been ungodly awful.

"So nice she could come for a visit," Mother continued.

Nice like head lice or burnt coffee or a day wasted in a hospital bed.

"I'm glad you met her," Anarchy replied. "You two have so much in common."

Mother's nostrils flared.

"Strong women dedicated to their children's happiness." Nice save. He made interfering sound like a positive.

Mother sniffed. "I let Ellison lead her own life."

Three jaws dropped. None of them Mother's.

I recovered first. "Very enlightened of you, Mother." I took a quick breath. "There's a possibility the car accident was deliberate. Anarchy's going to stay with me for a few days."

Now Mother's jaw dropped. Was she shocked by the murder attempt or the man not my husband staying at my house?

Before she could argue I turned to Grace. "Would you do me a favor?"

"Of course."

"Call Jinx and let her know I'm in the hospital."

Grace tilted her head. "Jinx?"

"Yes."

"Not Libba?"

"Call her too, but call Jinx first."

Mother's eyes narrowed. "What are you up to?"

"If I'm spending a day here, my friends may want to visit."

Jinx would be here in a flash—motivated by concern and her ongoing goal of being first to collect newsworthy items. If she hadn't married George, she'd have been a Pulitzer prize-winning investigative journalist. Or a Hollywood reporter. Probably a Hollywood reporter.

"Jinx will gossip."

I was counting on it. I'd hear all about Lucinda's luncheon and Jinx's impressions of Monica Alexander.

The nurse bustled in with my coffee, spotted Mother, and paled.

I took the cup from her hands and sipped. "Thank you." Coffee might not hold the answers to life's questions, but it made those questions bearable.

A BOUQUET PROCEEDED JINX. Big. Filled with phlox and lilies and roses to counteract the hospital's antiseptic smells. Vibrant to cancel out the raw oatmeal walls. She positioned the flowers on the ledge in front of the plate-glass window and eyed me with interest. "How are you feeling?"

"I'll be fine. Thank you for the flowers. They're beautiful."

"You're lucky you didn't hurt your face."

"Lucky would be not getting hit."

"I suppose." Her eyes narrowed. "Where are you hurt?"

"My shoulder and hip." The bruises looked like spilled ink —large and black and messy. "And my head."

"The driver didn't stop?"

"No."

"A kid joyriding?"

"Maybe. Maybe Prudence."

Jinx's answering smile was filled with evil glee. "I heard the police questioned her and checked her car."

"And?"

"No dents."

I sighed.

"You've had quite a week."

"That's an understatement."

"I heard the body in your study was Monica Alexander."

How kind of Jinx to give me an opening. "Yes. Did you—"

"She'd been shot?"

"No. How well—"

"Stabbed?"

"No. Did you—"

"Strangled?"

Obviously, I wasn't meant to ask questions. "Bee sting."

"Bee sting?" Her brows lifted and her eyes glinted. "You mean it was an accident?"

"You sound surprised."

"Your track record suggests murder. Although I shouldn't be surprised about the bee. She was deathly allergic."

"How did you know that?"

"I remember from college. We were friends. Not best friends. But friends."

"Did you stay close?" Jinx had never mentioned Monica.

"When George and I went to Chicago, we had dinner with her and Monty. If they came here, the same. Other than that, Christmas and birthday cards."

"What was she like?" Why had she claimed Anarchy's name?

"She had a good heart. She volunteered."

I rolled my eyes. We all volunteered. Even Prudence.

"No," Jinx insisted. "She really did. She was a docent at the museum, spent countless hours at a children's hospital, visited lonely old people, even took them meals, and raised money for the arts. She didn't do it to get her name in a program or recognition. She genuinely cared."

"What about her husband?"

"Monty?" Jinx's laser gaze settled on my face.

I kept my expression neutral.

"He's some kind of consultant."

That I knew. I waited for more.

"He's never been my favorite."

"Oh?"

"No concrete reason. He just rubs me the wrong way. Also, he was convinced she was running around."

"Was she?"

""Not sure. My first thought is she didn't have the time. But Monty was convinced."

"What did you talk about at your luncheon?"

"The usual—husbands, kids, our friends from college."

"Did anything strike you as odd?"

"You said she died of a bee sting."

"She did."

"So why are you asking about her?" Jinx's eyes narrowed. "Someone nearly killed you last night. Coincidence?"

"I don't know." An honest answer. "The luncheon?"

"We arrived, a waiter served us iced tea and canapés, and we sat down to lunch. The table looked lovely. Lucinda used peonies from her garden. Amy wandered in. Poor lamb. She had a stomachache and was home from school. Lucinda sent her upstairs. Oh—Monica asked if we knew you."

"She did?"

"Apparently you have a friend in Lake Forest who told her about the bodies."

"What did you tell her?"

"That you were one of my dearest friends. Why was she at your house?"

"I don't know."

"I could ask around. Just the girls...do you suppose she knew someone who died in Lake Forest? Maybe she wanted your advice."

Had Anarchy considered that angle? "Jinx, I'm going to tell you something you can't repeat." I waited till she ran a finger across her lips and turned an imaginary key. "She told Aggie her name was Mrs. Anarchy Jones. How did she know about Anarchy?"

A flush darkened Jinx's cheeks. "I might have mentioned him."

"Oh?"

"You have to admit he's the best-looking man any of us have ever seen."

"Don't let George hear you say that."

"George already knows."

"Knock, knock."

We shifted our gazes to the door.

Lucinda Sandhurst stood inside the frame, holding a bowl of peonies and a box of chocolates. "Ellison, how are you feeling?"

I bit back my surprise. How long had she stood outside the door? What had she heard?

She stepped into the hospital room and added her peonies to the flowers on the window ledge.

"They're beautiful. Thank you."

"I'm afraid they're fading. The annuals soon will take over." In Kansas City, summer belonged to begonias and marigolds, geraniums and zinnias.

"How's Amy?" I asked.

"Much better." Lucinda smiled brightly.

"I'm so glad."

"She's a darling," added Jinx.

"The apple of her daddy's eye. He worries when she's not feeling well." Lucinda's gaze landed on me. "What happened? Where are you hurt?"

"My head, my shoulder, my hip. They'll let me go home tomorrow."

"What a relief. I've spent too much time in hospitals lately." Lucinda deposited the chocolates on the dresser. "And I can tell you, there's no place like home."

"Agreed."

"Congratulations are in order."

Jinx and I gaped at Lucinda.

"Bill told me he celebrated with you and your father."

"Oh. That."

"What?" Jinx demanded.

"She broke the ladies' club record," said Lucinda.

Jinx frowned at me. How had I failed to mention my golf score? "Does Piper know? Maybe she's the one who ran you down."

She wouldn't...actually, she would. I'd have to tell Anarchy.

"Hello." Liz Burkhart stood in the doorway. She smiled and stepped inside. "I hope I'm not interrupting. I brought you a little something." She handed me a package.

"Thank you." I unwrapped a box of watercolors, paintbrushes, and a small watercolor pad. It was the most thoughtful gift I'd ever received when stuck in a hospital bed. "I love it. I'll spend my afternoon painting the flowers Jinx and Lucinda brought me."

Jinx checked her watch. "Ellison, I must run. I'll call you tomorrow."

"Thank you for coming. And thank you for the flowers."

"I'll walk out with you," said Lucinda. "Ellison, feel better."

"Thank you for coming. And thank you for the flowers and chocolates."

"You're welcome."

Jinx and Lucinda left us, and Liz settled into the naugahyde chair. "How are you?"

"Sore. How are you?" The last time we'd talked she'd opened a vein.

"I took your advice."

I purposefully hadn't offered advice. "Oh?"

"You gave me the courage to talk to Randal about what I wanted. And since it didn't involve couples' therapy, he gave his blessing." She patted her palms together and grinned. "When I was in school, I loved chemistry, but I didn't want to teach."

"Aren't there jobs in chemistry?"

She frowned. "For women? Name a woman scientist."

I thought. Hard. "Marie Curie!" Triumph laced my tone. Although if she asked me what Marie Curie did, my ignorance would be all too apparent.

"When I was young, the idea of making my way in a man's field was too intimidating. Now? Now, I want to back to school. I want a degree in chemical engineering."

Science and math—it sounded like my own personal hell.

"Randal said if school makes me happy, he's all for it."

"He won't mind when you study instead of cooking dinner, when you write a paper instead of ironing his shirts?"

"He says he won't." Her grin widened. "I love being a wife and mother, but that can't be all I am. You understand."

"I do." I also understood, when she got her degree, she'd want to use it. Randal might wish he'd opted for therapy when his wife worked the same hours he did.

Liz was poised to wander far from the life plan her parents and teachers provided. She'd tried their plan. She'd married a nice man, a good provider. She'd produced children. She had cocktails at the club on Friday evenings and vacationed in Martha's Vineyard. She should be grateful. Instead, she wanted more. Randal might give her his blessing, but had he thought through the changes coming his way?

"I told Randal how helpful you were."

I added Liz's husband to the list of people who might want to run me down.

Chapter Ten

The hospital refused to let me leave on a Sunday. Instead of going home, I spent the day painting watercolor portraits of the nurses and still lifes of the flowers on the sill.

Libba picked me up at eleven on Monday. "I agree with Frances. You need to stop with the frequent trips to the hospital."

It wasn't as if I enjoyed hospitals. Quite the opposite. The smells—the metallic tang of blood, the cloying sweetness of urine, the sharp bite of iodine and cleaning products—were disgusting. The gowns with their open backs and ridiculous ties and snaps were designed to embarrass the wearer. The sheets were scratchy and the mattresses hard. Worst of all, the coffee never tasted as good as Mr. Coffee's. "You win. I'll stay away."

She grinned at me. "Cranky?"

Who could blame me? "I'm hungry." Hospital food was terrible—I could make a more appetizing meal.

"Winstead's?"

"Please."

She drove us to my favorite hamburger spot, and we slid

into a fifties-style booth, ignored the menus, and waved at Grace's favorite waitress, Ruby.

Ruby's uniform was the same shade of mint as the booths and the menus. She pulled her order pad from the pocket of a simple white apron that protected her from spills. "The usual?"

I nodded. "Please."

"For you, ma'am?"

Libba scowled at the "ma'am," yanked a paper napkin from the chrome-plated dispenser, and stemmed the flow of water from a sweating glass. "A steakburger with everything, fries, and a small frosty malt."

Ruby made a note on her pad. "That'll be right out."

Libba watched her walk away. "Why does she remember your order and not mine?"

"Grace and I have eaten a meal here at least once a week for fifteen years." Also, I tipped better.

"Hmph."

"Thank you for picking me up." I leaned against the back of the booth and resisted closing my eyes. Getting hit by a car took a lot out of a woman, and I needed a nap.

"So, why did I get to pick you up? Where's Frances?"

"Pouting."

"Oh?"

"She's furious with me. Also, she has a bridge game."

"Why is she angry?"

"Anarchy is worried about me. He'll be staying in the guest room."

Libba waggled her brows. "The guest room?"

"Yes." My tone should have ended that line of questioning, but I was talking to Libba; tone had no bearing.

She shook her head sadly, as if I'd somehow disappointed her. "You still haven't—"

"Libba," I warned. We would not discuss my sex life in a booth at Winstead's.

"What are you waiting for? You're not getting any younger, and it's obvious you want to."

"Obvious?"

She smirked at me. "You undress him with your eyes."

"I do not." Did I?

"Yes, you do. He does the same to you."

"He does?"

The smirk grew. "I'm surprised you've kept your hands off each other this long. If it were me, I'd have hopped into bed with him months ago. You should do that. Sooner rather than later."

"Ellison, I heard you were in an accident. How are you?" June Shay wore a seersucker dress, a Nantucket basket over her arm, an unfortunate shade of frosted pink on her lips, and a slightly shocked expression. Obviously she'd overheard Libba's advice.

"Thank you for asking. I'm a bit sore, but I'll be fine."

June smiled at me as if I'd given her the best news she'd ever heard. "I must tell you, Piper is beside herself." Piper Osborne and June were sisters, and their relationship made the up-down-and-all-around connection I had with my sister, Marjorie, look stable and easy. "She wants a one-on-one round."

"I won't be golfing anytime soon. I dislocated my shoulder." Did June not see the sling?

"Piper's held that record for seven years."

I shrugged and wished I hadn't when my shoulder twanged. "I had a lucky day."

"I'll say." She leaned forward and whispered, "Please, let me buy your lunch."

What? She wasn't upset? "You don't need to—"

She straightened but kept her voice low. "You have no idea what holidays are like. We relive every hole of her record round. Every single holiday."

"That can't be fun." Libba's sympathetic grimace hid a smile.

"The best Christmas we've had in years was when Uncle Brud's angina flared. We spent the whole day at the hospital."

I weighed the hospital's horrible smells, bad food, and sub-par coffee against Piper's memories and offered a rueful smile. "Yikes."

"God love Uncle Brud, I'm fairly certain he faked the attack. You've done the family a tremendous favor. Piper's too competitive for her own good. Please, tell everyone you got lucky—that you didn't spend every day on the golf course for years. Please, tell them it didn't take much effort to beat her record."

"The record did stand for seven years."

"A fluke."

Ruby arrived carrying a large tray. She served us steak-burgers wrapped in wax paper, crispy fries, crispier onion rings, Libba's frosty, and my limeade. "Anything else?"

"Not right now. Thanks, Ruby."

"Ruby," said June, "I'll take the check."

"Thank you, June."

"No. Thank you. Enjoy your lunch." She left us and returned to a booth on the other side of the restaurant.

Libba lifted a fry and leaned forward. "If Piper was as bad as she says, June got off cheap."

I stirred the lime sherbet into my limeade with the bright red straw. If Piper was as bad as June said, would she do something to remove the competition?

∼

MOTHER'S MERCEDES sat in the circle drive in front of my house.

I turned to Libba. "Want to go shopping?"

"I'm not dressed for shopping." Excuses, excuses.

"I'll buy you something to wear."

Her eyes sparkled. "Coward."

"Easy for you to say. She's not your mother. You can drop me off and drive away."

"It's your fault," Libba replied. "You're the one who told her Anarchy was moving in."

"He's not moving in. He's staying for a few days. And believe me, it's better I tell her than she hear his car was here overnight from the neighbors."

Libba shifted to park and opened her door. We weren't leaving. Drat.

"I thought you were my friend."

"I am, but I like a good show. Maybe Max will protect you."

"Even Max is afraid of Mother."

"If it gets too bad, tell her you need to rest. Go." She shooed me toward the front door. "I'll carry in your things."

"Ellison Walford Russell." Mother met me in the foyer. "Where have you been?"

"Libba and I went to lunch at Winstead's."

Libba, camouflaged by Jinx's bouquet, slipped past Mother's glare.

"I practically kicked out my bridge group so I could be here and see you settled." The club was closed on Mondays, so Mother's Monday bridge game round-robined between the players' houses.

"I didn't realize you'd be here."

She huffed. "Has he moved in yet?"

No need to ask who. "Anarchy?"

She pressed her hands against her heart as if I'd wounded her.

Libba sneaked through the foyer to get a second load of flowers from her car.

"No. He's not here. Yet."

"People will talk."

People always talked. "Someone ran me down, and you're worried about gossip?"

Mother's lips pursed as if she'd eaten a lemon.

"I was going to Italy with him. No one will be shocked if he spends the night."

"Grace is here!"

"And Anarchy will be in the guest room."

Libba hurried past us with the bowl of peonies shielding her face and the watercolor pad tucked beneath her arm.

"Can't he just figure out who hit you?"

"He's trying."

"Tell him to try harder."

Libba slinked halfway through the foyer before Mother caught her. But rather than comment on the deep vee of Libba's t-shirt or the tightness of her jeans, Mother appealed to her. "Tell her."

Libba was rightfully wary. "Tell her what?"

"Anarchy doesn't need to stay here. It's not decent. Besides, Ellison won't be alone. Grace is here. And Aggie." Mother once told me Libba had the morals of a call girl (Libba didn't equate sex with commitment—an anathema to Mother). Mother's plea revealed her deep desperation—she'd try any port in this Anarchy storm.

Libba tiptoed toward the door as if she'd been dropped in a minefield and not my foyer. "We both know Ellison will set a good example for Grace."

"That doesn't matter. How it looks matters."

"What I do doesn't matter?" I couldn't keep the smile from my lips. "So you're okay with Anarchy and me sharing a bed?"

"Don't be fresh, Ellison." In the kitchen, the flowers wilted from the chill in her voice.

Ding, dong.

Saved by the bell.

Libba pulled open the front door.

Helen Winston stood on the stoop. She held a Swedish ivy in a canary-yellow cache pot and wore a polite smile.

"Helen!" I exclaimed. "How nice to see you. Please, come in." I pulled her into my home.

Helen blinked, surprised by my enthusiasm. "I heard you were hit by a car and wanted to let you know I was thinking of you."

"How kind. May I offer you coffee?" Please, please, please.

"I shouldn't. You need your rest."

"I'll sit. I'll rest. We'll let Libba push Mr. Coffee's button."

Libba grinned. "I love pushing buttons." Boy, did she.

I refrained from rolling my eyes. Barely. "Shall we sit?" I led Helen and Mother toward the living room. "Helen, you know my mother, Frances Walford?"

"Of course. So nice to see you, Mrs. Walford."

Mother had been auditioning girls (now women) for the role of my best friend since Libba taught me, Tommy Sayers, and Bill Thorne to play Spin the Bottle when we were twelve. She smiled approvingly at my friend who was appropriately married, presumably faithful, and didn't advertise her cleavage before seven o'clock in the evening. "Thank you for thinking of Ellison."

"She did me a tremendous favor last week."

Not so tremendous. All I'd done was sub bridge. "I was happy to help."

"Speaking of help—" Mother's gaze raked across my immaculate living room "—where's Aggie?"

"Given that Max isn't here, I assume she's walking him."

"Probably for the best." Mother smiled at Helen. "Ellison's dogs have no manners."

"My Fritz causes so much trouble."

"Fritz? What breed?" asked Mother.

"A Schnauzer."

"Aggie made cookies." Libba stood in the doorway with a tray. In deference to Mother, she'd poured the coffee into a carafe and found cups and saucers rather than mugs. "Chocolate chip."

"Ellison's housekeeper is a gem. Hunter Tafft found her."

Libba put the tray on the coffee table, and we exchanged a Mother-will-never-give-up-on-Hunter look.

"Aggie's a phenomenal baker." I picked up the carafe. "How do you like your coffee, Helen?"

"Black."

I poured, added a cookie to the saucer's edge, and handed her the cup.

"Coffee, Mother?"

"Please. Cream, no sugar."

I readied Mother's coffee. "Libba?"

"Just a cookie." She grabbed one from the plate, bit, and moaned—a low, sexy moan. "These are orgasmic."

Mother's face was stone. No reaction. But I saw the white in her knuckles where she gripped the chair's arm. "Helen, are you still involved with the garden club?"

"I am." Helen sipped her coffee and took a bite of her cookie. She didn't moan.

Mother smiled her approval. "I always enjoy the garden tour. So many good ideas."

Mother didn't garden. She hired landscapers. She hired gardeners. Any "ideas" in her yard came from them.

Libba reached for another cookie.

"Harrington and I visited Winterthur last year. Such gorgeous gardens."

I bit my tongue. Mother and Daddy visited the museum to view the Colonial antiques, not the gardens.

Helen took another bite of cookie. "I've always wanted to go. Maybe when the children are gone."

"How old are they?" Mother inquired.

"Fifteen and twelve." Helen rubbed her throat. "Ellison, does your housekeeper put nuts in her cookies?"

"Not usually. Why?"

"I'm allergic." A deep flush darkened Helen's suddenly puffy cheeks.

"How allergic?"

Helen held up her hands. Fat sausages had replaced her fingers. "I should probably go to the hospital."

Mother shot me a now-you've-done-it-you've-killed-this-nice-woman-who-should-replace-Libba-as-your-best-friend scowl.

I pushed out of my chair. "I'll call an ambulance."

"My purse," Helen wheezed. "There's a kit."

Libba ripped open Helen's purse, sent a brush and lipstick halfway across the room in her haste, and pulled out a plastic box. "This?"

Helen, whose lips now took up the bottom half of her face, nodded.

"What do we do?"

"Shot," Helen croaked.

Libba pried open the box and stared. "It's a needle."

"That's what they use for shots," I snapped.

"I hate needles."

Oh dear Lord. "Let me." I held out a shaking hand.

"No. I'll do it."

Libba jabbed the syringe into a vial and pulled out the plunger. "Where?"

"Leg." Helen's voice was faint and her skin a distressing shade of lavender.

Libba injected Helen's leg.

Helen relaxed, and her eyes fluttered shut.

"Is she dead?" Mother demanded. "I swear to you, Ellison, if there's another death in this house this week, I'll—"

"She's not dead," I snapped. Please let her not be dead. I dashed across the hall, picked up the phone, and called for help.

Libba and I followed the ambulance to the hospital.

"You made it less than three hours," she said.

I dragged my gaze from the ambulance's taillights and looked at her. "Pardon?"

"At eleven o'clock, you promised you'd avoid hospitals. It's not yet two."

"You sound like Mother."

"No need to be cruel. It was just an observation."

"You're sure you're not filling the pick-on-Ellison void?" Mother had opted not to come with us.

"Very funny."

I thought so.

Libba parked, and we shuffled into the emergency room, sat in uncomfortable, molded plastic and naugahyde chairs, and waited for Helen's husband.

Libba jumped up when Al rushed through the doors.

My bruised hip ached, and I rose more slowly.

"Al!" she called.

He hurried to us. "What happened?"

"Ellison served cookies with nuts."

I refrained from jabbing Benedict Arnold with my elbow. "I'm so sorry, Al."

He waved away my apology. "Is she okay?"

"I gave her a shot," said Libba.

"Thank God you were there. You probably saved her life." He turned to me. "You didn't warn her about the nuts?"

"No. I didn't know she's allergic, and my housekeeper doesn't usually include them." Also, Helen hadn't asked.

Al scowled, straightened his tie, and marched up to the check-in desk without replying.

I sank into the uncomfortable chair. "I feel awful."

"She'll be fine." Libba dismissed my feelings. "I'm just glad she had that kit."

"Me too." Without that syringe and vial, Helen might be dead in my living room. "She didn't have one."

"Yes, she did."

"I'm not talking about Helen."

"Who?"

"Monica Alexander didn't have a kit." Her purse's contents had covered the study floor—wallet, lipstick, handkerchief, comb—but no syringe, no vial.

"Maybe she didn't carry one."

I frowned. "If you were allergic to bee venom, wouldn't you carry a kit during the months they're active?"

"Yes."

"So, where's the kit?"

"Are you saying someone took it?"

"I don't know. But if she carried a kit, and it wasn't there when she needed it, her death seems like murder." I pushed out of the chair, ignoring the sharp pain in my hip.

"Where are you going?"

"To call Anarchy." I stumbled toward the payphone.

"Sit. I'll call him." Libba's hand closed around my arm. "You look as if you'll drop any second."

"You do care."

"Yeah, but don't push your luck."

A man rushed past us, nearly knocking us flat.

I stared after him. "Is that Bill Sandhurst?"

Libba looked over her shoulder. "Yes."

"Oh, no." I leaned against the nearest wall and waited for my knees to firm.

"What's wrong?" Libba demanded. "What now?"

"Bill had a child in his arms."

Chapter Eleven

I followed Bill to the check-in, where a nurse took Amy from his arms and disappeared behind swinging doors.

"What's her name?" asked the woman behind the desk.

Bill gaped at his arms as if he couldn't wrap his mind around their emptiness.

"Amy," I said. "Amy Sandhurst."

"Has she been a patient here before?"

That I couldn't answer. "Bill?"

"Yes. No." Bill raked his fingers through his hair and his chin quivered. "I don't know." He regarded me without a shred of recognition. I saw the moment he connected Harrington Walford's daughter with the woman standing next to him. "Ellison?"

"Bill, what happened?"

"The school called. They said Amy was sick and they couldn't reach Lucinda. I picked up Amy, and she passed out in the car. I drove straight here." He glanced around the waiting room. "This was the closest hospital."

But the children's hospital had her records. I patted his arm. "You did the right thing. Where's Lucinda?"

He frowned. "Somewhere on the Plaza. She's been through so much lately, I told her to buy herself new spring clothes." He rubbed the pads of his fingers across his cheekbones. "I don't know what happened. She was telling me her tummy ached and she just...faded."

"Mr. Sandhurst?"

Bill's head swiveled.

"You can come back now."

He left me without a second glance.

I hobbled back to my chair.

"What happened?" asked Libba.

"Amy's stomach."

She winced as if she empathized. "Anarchy's on his way."

"What? Why?"

"Because I told him you needed to talk to him—needed him —and you wouldn't leave the hospital till you knew Helen was okay."

I stared at Libba, ready to argue, but everything she'd told him was spot on. I needed to tell him about the missing kit. I needed him. And I wasn't leaving till I had assurances I hadn't killed Helen with chocolate chip cookies.

Libba reached her arms over her head and stretched. "When he gets here, I'm leaving."

"Why?"

"Your life is exhausting." She barely covered an enormous yawn. "I need a nap."

That made two of us. I hugged her with my good arm.

Ten minutes later, Anarchy pushed through the emergency-room doors. He paused, and his gaze searched the waiting room.

His shoulders relaxed when he spotted me, and the sharp expression in his eyes softened. He bounded toward us.

Libba stood, but Anarchy brushed past her. He leaned forward and his lips whispered across my forehead.

My tightly wound nerves loosened. "I'm glad you're here."

He sank into Libba's seat, took my hands, and stared into my eyes. "All you have to do is call. How's your friend?"

Libba cleared her throat, a half-amused, half-annoyed sound, and we both looked up. "I'm leaving. Don't do anything I wouldn't do."

I smiled my thanks at her. "That leaves us plenty of leeway."

She tapped her chin. "Don't get caught having sex in the supply closet."

Anarchy guffawed, and I felt the blood drain from my face. "Promise."

We watched her leave, and Anarchy settled in. "So, your friend?"

"She's being admitted." I took a breath and told him about Helen—the cookies, the kit, the shot in her leg. "Where was Monica's kit?"

He centered his elbows on his knees and lowered his head to his hands. "The medical examiner released her body this morning. She's on her way to Chicago. Damn. I wish I knew if she carried a kit."

"We could call Monty," I suggested. "Ask if she carried one."

"We could pay him a visit."

"In Chicago?"

"Why not?"

Why not? "If we left in the morning, we could catch a late afternoon flight home."

"We could spend the night."

My heart stuttered.

"It's not Venice, but it might be good to get away." He waited for my answer and bit the corner of his lower lip as if he were nervous.

"Where would we stay?"

"A hotel."

Me. Anarchy. Alone. No dogs. No daughter. No mothers. No murder. "I wouldn't mind popping in to Marshall Fields."

"So you'll go?"

The grin rising from my chest couldn't be denied. "Yes."

His hand tightened around mine, a secure anchor in a stormy sea, and I took a deep breath.

Before I could exhale, Bill stumbled into the waiting room. His tie hung askew and his cheeks were as white as his shirt.

I stood. "What did the doctor say?"

"He's not sure what's wrong." Deep lines etched Bill's forehead and the corners of his eyes drooped. "I need to call Lucinda—let her know where we are."

I pointed. "The payphones are around the corner."

Bill lurched away, his shoulders bent beneath three tons of worry.

"Your friend's husband?" Anarchy asked.

"No. I'm sorry. I should have introduced you. That's Bill Sandhurst. His little girl is sick."

"Little girl?"

I glanced at the hallway where Bill had disappeared. "She's in third grade."

"But he's—"

"At least sixty. Second family."

"How old is his wife?"

"Three years younger than I am."

"She married for money?"

"Good guess, but no. But she might have daddy issues."

There were limited reasons why a woman married a man twenty-five years her senior.

When Bill came round the corner, I studied him. He was fit. He had craggy good looks. He still had his hair. Was I being unfair to Lucinda? To Bill? They'd weathered a storm when he married one of his daughter's friends. The ladies around the bridge table gave the marriage six months. But fifteen years had passed, and they remained together.

Bill waved at me. "I left a message on our machine. I hope she gets it." He disappeared into the treatment area. I resumed my seat.

People trickled in—a woman with a broken arm, a teenager with a bloody gash above his eye (he mentioned a skateboard as his mother wrung her hands), and a man with chest pains. Seconds lasted minutes, and minutes lasted hours. What I knew about physics would fit on a postage stamp, but I was fairly certain Einstein's space-time continuum had overlooked the way time morphed into slow molasses in hospitals. Through it all, Anarchy held my hand.

Finally, when there was a break in the action, I approached the woman at the front desk. "Could you tell me please, how is Mrs. Winston?"

"I'll find out for you, Mrs. Russell." She knew my name. I never set out for everyone who worked the ER to know me, but here we were—and on days like this familiarity was darned useful.

The woman—Janet, according to her nametag—reappeared a moment later. "Doctor is admitting her."

"It's serious?"

"He wants to keep an eye on her."

"And Amy Sandhurst, how is she?"

"I'll have to ask the doctor." She looked over my shoulder

and offered me an apologetic smile. "Would you please step aside?"

I shifted, and a woman with her arms wrapped around her middle limped forward. "I fell again."

Janet's eyes narrowed. "Is your husband with you, Mrs. Parker?"

"No."

"You're sure I can't call the police?"

"I fell," the woman insisted. "I messed up some ribs."

Janet sighed. "We have paperwork."

The woman, Mrs. Parker, nodded as if she were all too familiar with hospital paperwork.

I returned to Anarchy. "That woman—" I nodded toward Mrs. Parker "—her husband hurt her."

He sat straighter. "Did she say that?"

"She said she fell."

Anarchy slumped. "I can't do anything unless she says he hurt her."

"But—"

"I know." His face was grim. "Fear and love and pain get mixed up. Victims refuse to accuse their abusers. Even when it might save them. It's frustrating."

"But—"

"I can't make her press charges. I can't make her leave."

Anarchy couldn't right all the world's wrongs. I knew that. "I wish..."

He took my hand and pulled me gently into the chair next to his. "I wish for the same thing. How's your friend?"

"They're keeping her for observation."

Al Winston stepped into the waiting room and spotted me. "You're still here." He sounded surprised.

"How's Helen?"

"She'd like to see you before they take her upstairs."

"Of course." I glanced at Anarchy. "I'll be back in a few minutes."

"I'll be right here."

I struggled to my feet—each time I stood it required more effort—and Al led me to the cubicle where they'd treated Helen.

I stuck my head inside. "Hi."

The swelling in Helen's face had subsided, and she managed a small smile. "Thank you for getting me here so quickly."

"That was the ambulance. Helen, I feel terrible about the cookies."

"How were you to know? I should have asked." She sighed. "Is Al with you?"

"He's down the hall talking to a doctor."

"Poor man. He was so worried. This hasn't happened in years. Last time it happened, we were at his mother's. She put pecans in the Thanksgiving dressing and I nearly died. She did it on purpose."

"That'll sour a relationship."

She laughed, then winced as if the small chuckle hurt her. "She knew I was allergic." Helen shook her head. "To this day, she claims she thought I was only allergic to peanuts."

Wow. At least Celeste hadn't attempted murder. Then again, Anarchy and I weren't married.

"I promise, the cookies weren't on purpose. Do you always carry a kit?"

"Always. I never leave home without it."

Al joined us. "They're taking you upstairs. I arranged for a private room."

Helen smiled at her husband. "You take such good care of me."

"Helen, again, I'm so sorry."

Al snorted as if my apology fell short of the mark.

"Not your fault," said Helen. "How could you know? Don't give it another thought."

An orderly appeared and wheeled Helen away. Al gave me a terse nod and followed.

I walked back to the waiting room and found Anarchy still in the uncomfortable chair. He stood and wrapped an arm around my shoulders. "You okay?"

"Helen said something, and it made me realize—Jinx knew."

"Jinx knew what?"

"Jinx knew Monica was allergic to bee venom."

He tilted his head. "You don't think Jinx—"

"No. No. Of course not." I stared at Anarchy's chest. "Jinx and Monica weren't the best of friends, but Jinx knew about Monica's allergy."

"And?"

I lifted my gaze to his eyes. "Who else knew?"

"You think someone murdered her?"

I nodded.

He sighed. "C'mon, I'll drive us home."

Anarchy parked behind the house (a hidden car would thwart Marian Dixon's nosiness), and we entered through the back door.

Grace sat at the kitchen island with an algebra book open in front of her. Aggie washed lettuce at the sink. Max lounged. They all looked at us when we walked in.

"Where have you been?" Grace sounded disturbingly like Mother.

"The hospital."

"They released you this morning." She definitely sounded like Mother.

"I went back."

"What?"

I held up my hands. "I'm fine."

"We got home and found a strange car in the drive and the living room a mess. The neighbors talked about an ambulance —" Grace closed her book and crossed her arms "—

and you were nowhere to be found."

"There was a small mishap." If nearly killing someone with cookies could be called a mishap.

"Oh?" Grace even tilted her head like Mother.

Helen's near-death reaction to the cookies wasn't Aggie's fault, but would Aggie agree? "I served the cookies."

Aggie blinked. "Did you like them? I used a new recipe." She frowned. "Did someone choke? I used walnuts..."

"Helen Winston had a small reaction, and we took her to the hospital."

Aggie's hands covered her mouth and her eyes widened.

"She's fine. Really."

Aggie didn't look convinced.

Grace turned to Anarchy. "How long are you staying with us?" Her tone was pure Mother, but the concern creasing her face said she wanted him here.

"Till we figure out who hit your mother."

She nodded her approval of his plan. "Any suspects?"

"Not really."

"Who have you annoyed lately?" Grace demanded.

"Young lady, watch your tone." I wanted my daughter back. I already had a mother—one who was more than I could handle.

"Who?" she asked with her own voice. "I'm worried."

"Piper Osborne," I offered.

Anarchy raised a brow. "Who?"

"I beat her course record," I explained.

Grace nodded and jotted Piper's name on a sheet of note-book paper. "What about Miss Davies?"

"We cleared her," Anarchy replied.

Grace frowned and rubbed her chin. "Did your mother rent a car?"

Was she suggesting Anarchy's mother had run me down?

"Yes. Why?"

"She's not one of Mom's fans."

"Grace!"

"What? She came here and threatened you." She glanced at Anarchy and shrugged. "Sorry, but it's true."

"She didn't threaten me. She warned me. And there's a world of difference between a warning and attempted manslaughter."

Anarchy stiffened. "What did she say?"

"She said I was shallow." I shrugged as if Celeste's opinion didn't matter.

"What else?"

"I'm not good enough for you."

His eyes narrowed. "And?"

"And she told me to stay away from you."

"And you told her?"

"I told her no."

"I don't get why she doesn't like Mom. Everyone likes Mom. Well, not Miss Davies. But everyone else. Even the people who don't like her pretend to."

I stared at the stranger inhabiting my daughter's body. "What are you talking about?"

"There are tons of people who get off on claiming famous people as friends."

"I'm not famous."

"Yes, you are."

"In a small world."

"A bigger world than they'll ever know."

Grace had a point. On my desk a stack of invitations (many from people I barely knew) awaited my reply.

She turned to Anarchy. "You didn't answer my question."

He blinked. "Which was?"

"Why doesn't your mother like Mom?" Grace was being incredibly rude. I should send her to her room. But I didn't. I wanted to hear his answer.

"My mother is difficult."

Grace treated to him to a heavy eye roll.

"My father was always busy at the university, and my brother, my sister, and I were her whole world. It's hard for her to let go."

"Um...you're like forty."

"Grace!"

Now I got an eye roll. "What? It's true."

"Parenting is hard." The understatement of the decade.

"I sort of get it if a kid's at home. Peggy's mother's life revolves around her. But when we graduate high school and go to college, she'll find a new hobby—play more golf or tennis, take up pottery, something. When Peggy's forty, her mother will be busy traveling to Boca or spoiling her grandchildren, not interfering in Peggy's life."

"Doesn't always work that way." My voice was dry.

Grace ceded my point with a wince. "Fine. But that doesn't explain why Mrs. Jones doesn't like you."

"She doesn't have to like me. Celeste didn't run me over to keep me from dating her son."

"Then who?" Grace tapped the paper that still held only one name. "I hate it when people hurt you. I want it to stop!"

"We all do." Anarchy's voice was gentle, as if he didn't care Grace had accused his mother of attempted murder.

I hobbled to a stool and sat.

Aggie, who'd followed our exchange in silence, spoke. "What can I get you? Coffee?"

I glanced at the kitchen clock. "Maybe after dinner. Right now, I'd love a glass of wine."

"This is serious, Mom."

"I know. Anarchy will catch whoever hit me."

"He doesn't have any suspects."

"Can we talk about this later? I'm tired. I'm sore. And I'm perfectly safe."

Grace's eyes narrowed. "For tonight. What about tomorrow?"

"Anarchy and I are going to Chicago for a day or two."

"You are?"

"If Aggie doesn't mind staying with you."

Aggie set a glass of white wine in front of me and squeezed my good shoulder. "Of course I don't mind. I'd planned on being here for your trip to Italy."

"Why Chicago?"

"I haven't been to Marshall Fields in an age." True, but not the truth.

"Why, Mom?"

I wouldn't lie to Grace. "We're going to see Monty Alexander."

"Why?"

"Because I think Monica was murdered."

Chapter Twelve

I slept well knowing Anarchy was down the hall and woke up feeling refreshed. There was a spring in my step as I descended the stairs for my morning rendezvous with Mr. Coffee.

You look as if you're feeling better.

"I am." I checked his reservoir (Aggie had filled it), eyeballed the level of grounds in his filter, and pushed his button.

I'm glad.

"What a week."

I know it's been rough. I'll always be here for you.

"What would I do without you?"

"Are you talking to Mr. Coffee?"

I whirled around and found a grinning Anarchy. "Maybe."

"Maybe?"

"Yes," I admitted. "We chat every morning."

"About?"

"Whatever's on my mind."

"What's on your mind today?"

"Reservations for Chicago. The Drake or Palmer House?"

"You decide." He stepped closer to me. "Anything else?"

"Was Monica murdered? Who tried to kill me? How's Helen? How's Amy? When did Grace develop a mile-wide Frances Walford streak?"

He stepped closer still.

My heart stuttered.

"What else?" His voice weakened my knees.

I clutched the counter's edge. "Will Mother's head explode when she finds out we traveled to Chicago?"

"You're telling her?"

"There are no secrets from Mother."

His finger grazed my jawbone.

Sweet nine-pound baby Jesus, that felt good. I tilted my head and gazed into coffee-brown eyes.

"What else?" he whispered.

A breath separated us. If I inhaled deeply, our chests would touch. My brain, admittedly not at its best before coffee, browned out. Not a single coherent thought rose to its surface. "Don't you talk to your coffee maker?"

He grinned. His eyes sparkled.

Only my white-knuckled grip on the counter kept me standing.

"I don't talk to appliances."

"You should," I whispered. "Some of them are quite intelligent."

Coffee's ready. If Mr. Coffee was jealous of the new man in my kitchen, he hid it well.

"Coffee," I croaked.

"In a minute." Anarchy's arms reached around my back and pulled me to him. One hand rose till he cradled my nape in his big, warm hand.

My lips parted.

Clop, clop, clop.

He jumped backward. "What is that? Do you have elephants?"

"It's Grace." I used both hands to clutch the counter. I needed the stability—a shot of lust before my morning arabica left me shaky.

"Hi, Mom!" She burst into the kitchen, took one look at me, and smirked. "Sorry. Didn't mean to interrupt."

"You weren't."

"Yeah." She rolled her eyes. "Right. Good morning, Anarchy."

"Good morning, Grace."

"Are you guys leaving today?"

"We have a few things to do this morning. Our flight leaves this afternoon."

"How long will you be there?"

I poured heaven into a mug. "We'll only be gone a couple of days ."

"Cool." She filled a bowl with Super Sugar Crisp and added milk. "What things?"

"When I was in the hospital, I did watercolors of the flowers on the sill. I thought I'd give them to the women who brought the flowers. Anarchy, do you want coffee?"

"Please."

"No investigating on your own?" Grace regarded me with narrowed eyes.

I poured a second cup. "No investigating. Cream? Sugar?"

"Black."

Grace's eyes narrowed to tiny slits. "No walks by yourself?"

Max lifted his head at the word "walk."

"Promise."

"Fine." She'd given her permission. Grudgingly. My daughter's Frances Walford streak was wider than a mile.

"Morning." Aggie, resplendent in an avocado-green kaftan

embroidered with orange thread, bustled through the kitchen with a basket of laundry in her arms. "Let me throw this in the washing machine, then I'll make omelets."

"Thank you," I called after her.

"Grace—" Aggie's voice carried from the laundry room "—I see you with that sugary cereal. It's not good for you."

Grace spooned another mouthful, abandoned her bowl in the sink, and grabbed her backpack. "The Drake or Palmer House?"

"I haven't decided."

"Palmer House. If you leave before I get home, will you call tonight?"

"Absolutely."

She kissed my cheek, waved at Anarchy, and dashed out the back door before Aggie could scold her further about her cereal choices.

"I need a shower." A cold one. I refilled my mug. "Would you please tell Aggie I'll be down in fifteen minutes?"

Anarchy's gaze caught mine over the rim of his mug and it was as if he could see straight into my soul. Lust. Nerves. Terror. Love. His lips curled. "I'll tell her."

Fifteen minutes later, dressed in a skirt embroidered with ladybugs (nothing sexy about ladybugs) and a white blouse with a Peter Pan collar, I paused in the doorway to the kitchen. Anarchy leaned against the counter. A pair of worn blue jeans clinging to his hips and a dark shirt speckled with water droplets said he'd showered even faster than I did.

My mouth went dry.

"More coffee?" Aggie asked.

Anarchy turned his gaze on me, and I barely managed a nod. "Please. What are you—" Since when did I squeak? "What are you doing this morning?"

"Taking the cat to a friend's. You?"

"I'm taking paintings to Liz, Lucinda, and Jinx."

His brows rose. "Jinx? You promised no investigating."

"If Jinx knew anything, she'd have called me."

"Sure about that?"

"Positive." Sort of.

We ate Denver omelets. We stared at each other like love-struck teenagers. We walked out the back door holding hands.

"Our flight leaves at two," he told me.

"I'll meet you back here in two hours."

He brushed a kiss across my lips and got in his car.

I drove to Jinx's house with a goofy grin on my face.

She answered the door in a floral bathrobe. "You're out and about early."

"I brought you something." I handed her the tube holding the painting.

"What is it? Come in. Coffee?"

"It's a small thank you for the lovely flowers." I followed her to the kitchen.

"Coffee?"

"Please."

She poured coffee into a mug decorated with trippy white mushrooms, opened the tube, spread the painting across her counter, and gasped. "Ellison, it's beautiful. Thank you."

"You're welcome. May I help myself to cream?"

"Of course." Jinx still stared at the watercolor. "I'll have this framed and hang it in the living room."

I poured cream into my coffee. "I'm glad you like it."

"Like it? I love it. I'm so glad you caught me."

"Caught you?"

"George and I are flying to Chicago at noon."

"You are?"

She nodded. "Monica Alexander's funeral is tomorrow morning."

I added a black dress to my packing list. "Maybe I'll see you there."

"You're going?"

"She did die in my house." And we had questions for her husband. "Listen, thanks for the coffee. I'll get out of your hair so you can get ready."

Jinx walked me to the door. "I love the painting. Thank you."

I gave her a quick hug. "Thanks for being such a good friend."

Next I drove to Liz's.

She answered the door with the look of a woman who'd barely made it out of the house for carpool. She wore wrinkled khakis, one of Randal's shirts with the sleeves rolled to her elbows, and her hair in a ponytail. "Ellison."

"Sorry to disturb your morning, but I used the paints you gave me and I have a painting for you."

"Seriously?" Her eyes lit with excitement.

I gave her the tube.

"Oh my gracious. This is amazing! Come in!"

She led me to the formal living room, pulled the painting from the tube, and unrolled its edges on her coffee table. "It's gorgeous! Thank you!"

"Thank you for the paints."

"It was nothing."

"They kept me entertained."

She glanced around her living room—Colonial antiques, plaid couches, the brass-and-glass coffee table—and frowned. "The sunroom is mine. No husband. No kids. I'll have this framed and hang it there."

"I'm glad you like it."

"I do!"

"Are things still okay with you and Randal?"

She smiled and nodded. "I wonder if we don't all take each other for granted."

"Pardon?"

"When Randal and I married, we were the centers of each other's worlds. Then came kids, and his career, and being a mom, and we stopped putting each other first. If nothing else, these past few days—my decision to return to school—reminded him I'm important." She blushed. "It's nice having his focus. May I offer you coffee?"

"Not today. I have a million errands." Just one more.

"You'll have to come over as soon as I get your painting hung."

"I'd like that."

"It's a date."

I left her, drove to Lucinda's, parked, rang the bell, and waited.

And waited.

I rang a second time. It was possible—even probable—the Sandhursts were at the hospital with Amy. I glanced at my watch, gave the closed door thirty seconds, and turned away.

"Mrs. Russell?"

I glanced over my shoulder.

The doorway framed Amy Sandhurst. She wore a lawn nightgown and clutched Oliver in her arms.

"Amy. You're home."

She nodded and offered me a worried smile. "I'm not supposed to answer the door, but I saw it was you."

"Where are your parents?"

"Daddy's at work. Mommy went to pick up medicine." She scrunched her nose.

"The doctors sent you home?"

"They don't know what's wrong." She looked as delicate as a flower, as pale as a wisp of moonlight.

"They're very smart men. I'm sure they'll figure it out."

Sweet little Amy rolled her eyes.

"This is for your mommy." I presented her with the tube.

"What is it?"

"A painting. Do you still want to come to my studio?"

A smile lit her face, transforming her from a sick child to a delighted pixie. "Yes, please."

"I'm going out of town for a few days. When I get back, I'll arrange it with your mommy."

"Okay."

"Should I stay with you till she gets home?"

"No. I should go to bed, so I can get better."

"I'll wait here till you lock the door."

Amy closed the door, and I heard the bolt slide into place. Poor kid.

ANARCHY HELD my hand as the plane took off. "You've been to Chicago before?"

I sighed happily as visions of summer clothes danced in my head. A Diane Von Furstenberg wrap dress did a cha-cha with a Missoni gown. A linen cover-up (perfect for poolside) rhumbaed with a wide-brimmed straw hat. "Michigan Avenue."

He tilted his head and frowned, as if my meaning escaped him.

"Michigan Avenue. The Magnificent Mile. The shopping is world class."

He squeezed my hand. "I should have guessed."

"Grace left a wish list on my pillow."

"I'm not surprised."

"Aggie has a birthday coming up. Maybe I can find her a Thea Porter kaftan."

"Nothing for you?" His eyes crinkled.

He knew better.

"We should drop off the bags and go directly to Marshall Fields."

He didn't react. Marshall Fields deserved a reaction.

"You've never been?"

"No."

"There's an endless atrium topped by a domed Tiffany ceiling. Very old world. Very elegant." My voice was dreamy, as if I were recounting a fairy tale with a happy ending. "It's the most beautiful store I've ever seen."

"More beautiful than Saks?"

"Yes."

"More beautiful than Neiman Marcus?"

"You're teasing me."

He leaned forward and kissed the corner of my mouth. "Maybe a little."

I ignored the way my insides went all tingly. "There's a gallery owner on State Street who called my agent about a show. I'd love to swing by and see his space."

"I thought we liked Michigan Avenue."

"We do, but State Street is good, too."

"Good to know."

"We could have a drink at the Walnut Room."

"Where?"

"The restaurant in Marshall Fields."

"If you'd like."

"We're staying near there."

"Grace picked the hotel."

"We have two favorites. The Drake is near Oak Street Beach, but Palmer House is within walking distance of Marshall Fields."

"I see the conundrum."

"Potter Palmer built the first Palmer House for his young bride."

"How young?"

"She was twenty-three years his junior." Older men marrying younger women was nothing new. "Thirteen days later, it burned in the Great Fire."

"They rebuilt."

"They rebuilt," I agreed. "And it's gorgeous."

"And close to your favorite store."

"Funny how that happens."

A second kiss tickled my lips, and I caught the woman across the aisle staring at us. I assumed she was jealous.

"We'll have to go to the funeral."

He nodded.

"I've never been to the Church of the Holy Spirit." But I could picture it. Soaring ceilings, wood paneling with an aged patina, sunlight streaming through a fortune in stained glass windows. It was, after all, in Lake Forest. "It will take us an hour to get there."

"I have a proposition for you."

My heart stuttered. "Oh?"

"When we leave the church, we forget about murder till we get back to Kansas City. I'll shop and visit your gallery and drink at the Pecan Room—"

"Walnut Room."

"Whatever."

I stopped him from saying anything else with a kiss. "What about tonight?"

"Tonight?" His eyes danced. "The guys told me we should eat pizza at Pequod's. They say the crust is caramelized."

"Pizza?" I'd been thinking of something entirely different. "I've never heard of Pequod's, but it sounds delicious."

"Delicious." His lips brushed against mine, and I forgot Marshall Fields, and Pequod's pizza, and my name.

The plane landed, we loaded Anarchy's hanging bag and my three suitcases into a taxi, and dropped everything at Palmer House. Then we climbed into a second taxi. After a thirty-minute ride, the cab dropped us in front of a nondescript brick building with a tired awning.

"This is it?"

Anarchy grinned.

Inside, the aromas of golden crust, oregano, tomato sauce, and melting cheese more than made up for the exposed brick walls, mismatched chairs, and shaky tables. I breathed deep.

Anarchy ordered at the counter, then joined me at a wobbly table with a street view. He held two frosted mugs and a pitcher of beer. "Old Style."

"What?"

"The beer, Ellison. It's Old Style."

"Is that a brewing technique?"

"A brand."

"Okay. What kind of pizza did you order?"

"Deep dish."

"I swear you're speaking a different language."

He grinned. "Sausage, peppers and onions with a deep-dish crust. I'm sure the Hazelnut Room is nice, but we need to expand your horizons."

"Walnut Room, and I'm here, aren't I?"

He clinked his beer mug against mine. "To expanding horizons."

Heat zinged through my whole body, and I took a large, cooling sip of Old Style.

Anarchy gazed out the window and frowned. "About my mother..."

Uh-oh. "What about her?"

"I'm sorry if she hurt your feelings."

Unbidden, tears prickled behind my eyes. "She's certain I'm wrong for you."

He rubbed the back of his neck.

"Now's the part when you tell me she's wrong. That I'm perfect for you. That meeting me is the best thing that ever happened to you."

A slow grin curled his lips. "Yes."

"Yes, what?"

"Yes to everything you said. It's all true."

I leaned back in my chair. "Then say it."

He reached across the table, claimed both my hands in one of his, and looked into my eyes. "You are the perfect woman. My mother's opinions don't matter. I love you just the way you are."

I melted into a puddle on Pequod's uneven floor. Anarchy deserved more than a puddle of goo—he deserved a response. "You're the best man I've ever known, and I count my lucky stars you're with me."

"And?" His eyes twinkled.

"I love you."

We stared across the table at each other. All I wanted was to be in his arms, to get lost in his kiss.

"Are you still hungry?" His voice was raw.

Nice to know I wasn't the only one affected. "We didn't drive halfway across Chicago to abandon our pizza before it arrives."

"We could get it to go."

"And eat it cold?"

"If I didn't know better, I'd assume you're avoiding going back to the hotel."

A slow smile curled my lips. "I'm not avoiding anything. It's just that you'll need your strength." Libba would be so proud.

A waiter brought out a blackened skillet that looked as if it had been salvaged from the Great Fire. Inside the pan, the cheese on our pizza still bubbled.

We ate quickly—burn-the-roof-of-my-mouth quickly.

We held hands on the much-too-long drive back to Palmer House.

Anarchy didn't seem to notice the hotel's soaring Art Deco ceilings or the 24-karat gold Tiffany chandeliers. Instead he jabbed at the up button till the elevator arrived.

We stepped inside. The car ascended. And I was suddenly filled with doubt. "It's been a while…"

He wrapped his arms around me, and his lips brushed against mine. "It's like riding a bike."

Oh, really? "Lots of fancy gears I won't use?"

He chuckled. "I don't know about fancy, but I promise you, we'll use every gear."

Heat flooded my cheeks. Any my chest. And other places.

He pulled me closer. "I also promise we'll go at whatever speed is best for you."

My mouth was too dry to answer.

He led me from the elevator, through the suite's living room, and into the bedroom.

And he was right about two things. It was like riding a bike (but *much* better). And we used every gear.

Chapter Thirteen

The Church of the Holy Spirit wasn't what I expected. It was understated rather than grand, with white walls, restrained windows, and dark-stained chairs instead of pews.

Anarchy and I sat near the back of the nave in the two seats farthest from the aisle.

Our fingers laced together.

A smile, entirely inappropriate for a funeral, was stuck on my face. Anarchy wore the same goofy expression.

The hotel-arranged car service had deposited us thirty minutes early, giving us the opportunity to watch the church fill with well-heeled mourners.

Anarchy glanced at his watch. "Would you excuse me a moment?"

"Of course." I let go of his fingers and closed my eyes, ready to visit last night's memories.

"Is this seat taken?" A woman in her mid-thirties stood next to me. She wore a navy wrap dress, carried a Gucci bag, and pointed to the free seat next to mine.

"No."

"Do you mind?"

"Of course not."

She sat and pulled a Kleenex from her Jackie. "Such a sad day."

I nodded my agreement.

"Did you know her well?"

"Not really." Not at all.

"I'm Lily." She held out her hand and gave me a surprisingly firm handshake.

"Ellison."

She took in my gray and lavender tweed Chanel suit (I was channeling Mother), Ferragamo pumps, and triple rope of pearls. "How did you know Monica?"

"She died at my house."

Lily gasped and her jaw dropped—for a half-second—then she snapped it closed. "It was nice of you to come." Questions burned in her eyes.

"Such a tragedy," I murmured. "You were friends?"

"Since kindergarten." She tilted her head and stared at the church's whitewashed ceiling. "I don't understand how this happened."

I didn't either. How did Monica's killer arrange for a bee sting?

"Tell me about her."

Lily lowered her head and bit her lower lip. She dabbed the Kleenex beneath her eyes. "She was amazing. The kindest woman you'd ever meet." She drew a ragged breath. "She genuinely cared about people."

"She sounds lovely."

"She was. She dedicated herself to helping sick children."

"I heard something about that."

"After Emma died..." Lily dabbed again.

"Emma?"

"She and Monty lost their daughter to cancer. After Emma passed, Monica became a tireless volunteer—at the kids' cancer agency and the children's hospital."

"I didn't realize they'd lost a child. I can't imagine." If anything happened to Grace, the loss would destroy me.

"In some ways, losing Emma made Monica stronger. She was an advocate for children's health, and not just here on the North Shore. She worked with hospitals in the city. She wanted every child to have a chance for a healthy life." Lily's gaze scanned the filling church. "Half the men here are doctors from the hospitals where she made a difference."

"I wish I'd known her."

"You would have liked her. Everyone did."

"As aware of health issues as she was, I'm surprised she didn't carry an allergy kit with her."

Lily frowned. "She did. Always. Monty even had a mono-grammed box made."

That stopped me. What had happened to Monica's kit? Had Monica noticed it was missing?

If someone took something out of my purse, would I notice?

Not till I needed it.

Monica had needed her kit. Desperately. Had she spent her last minutes digging through her purse for medicine that wasn't there?

She must have been terrified.

Jinx and George entered the church, and Jinx spotted me and raised her brows.

I waved back.

"Friends of yours?" asked Lily.

"Jinx is from Kansas City. She and Monica were at Sweet Briar together."

A watery smile touched Lily's lips. "Monica said something

about a lunch with her Sweet Briar friends. She so enjoyed all her trips to Kansas City."

"Lucinda, the hostess, is a friend. It sounded lovely."

Lily wiped her nose. "I'm glad. I can't believe she's gone. I still can't believe a bee sting killed her."

Neither could I.

Anarchy slid into his seat, and Lily's eyes widened (I didn't blame her—he looked incredibly handsome in a charcoal gray suit, crisp white shirt, and striped tie).

"Lily, this is Anarchy Jones. Anarchy, Lily was one of Monica's oldest friends."

Anarchy held out his hand. "Nice to meet you."

"Likewise."

Was she drooling?

Anarchy extracted his right hand from her grasp. His left hand found mine, and our fingers laced back together.

The organist began playing, and we fell silent.

My mind wandered during the service. To last night. To Anarchy. What came next for us? My mind shied away from the future. Instead, I thought about the woman who'd died in Henry's study. Did she have enemies? Who had wanted her dead? And why?

Had someone followed her from Chicago?

My responses to the funeral rites came by rote, and Anarchy tugged gently on my elbow when it was time to stand.

I glanced at Lily.

Tears streamed down her cheeks. She genuinely mourned her friend.

I felt a rush of sadness for Monica's loss. People had loved her, and they were hurting. At the front of the church, Monty openly sobbed. A friend supported him as they followed the priest up the aisle.

Lily wiped her eyes. "Are you going to the reception?"

I glanced at Anarchy, a question in my eyes. We'd made a deal. When we left the church, we'd forget about murder till we landed in Kansas City.

"It's at Monty's country club."

"Is the receiving line there?" I asked.

She nodded.

I swallowed a sigh. "We should pay our respects."

Anarchy gave a tiny nod. He agreed.

Lily wadded up her Kleenex and shoved the tissue into her bag. Then she turned over the program and tapped the paper with the tip of her manicured nail. "That's the address. I'll see you there." She eased out of the aisle.

"We don't have to go." We'd promised this time to each other. "We can go back to the city."

"Monica deserves justice."

He really was the best man I knew.

"Ellison!" Jinx and George had filed into the row in front of ours. "You're here! When did you decide to come?"

"At the last minute. You remember Anarchy?"

"Of course."

Anarchy and George shook hands.

"Are you going to the reception?" Jinx asked.

"Yes."

"Wonderful. We'll see you there."

I didn't care for the speculative expression on Jinx's clever face.

"C'mon, honey." George pulled her—and her unspoken questions—away.

"Jinx!"

She glanced over her shoulder at me.

"How often did Monica visit Kansas City?"

"Funny you should ask."

"Why?"

"I saw her on the Plaza a few weeks ago. She hadn't called, didn't let anyone know she was coming, and she didn't seem happy to see me." Jinx squinted as if she struggled for a clear view of the past. "Why do you ask?"

"No reason."

That earned me a searching gaze.

I waved at her. "See you at the reception."

"Interesting question." Anarchy's gaze was sharp. "What did you figure out?"

"Lily made it sound as if Monica traveled to Kansas City often. But according to Jinx, she didn't see her friends."

"The affair?"

I nodded.

"If we go to the reception, we may not make it to the Peanut Room." He was teasing. Again.

"The Walnut Room." Two could tease. "And you can forget about going there."

"Oh?"

"I'm not wasting a minute of our time together sipping overpriced cocktails in a pretty restaurant."

Heat flared in his eyes. He leaned forward and whispered against the shell of my ear, "We could go back to the hotel."

Yes. Yes. A thousand times yes. "We owe it to her to ask a few questions."

Disappointment (most gratifying) flashed across his face, but he tucked my hand into his arm and led me from the church.

Ray, our driver, opened the Town Car's back door for me. "Back to the city, Mr. Jones?"

"We've decided to stop by the reception." He gave Ray the program with the address printed on the back. "Can you get us there?"

The driver nodded. "Nice place."

I scooched across the seat and Anarchy got in next to me. Our fingers found each other immediately.

It would be so easy to forget the reception, return to Palmer House, and lock ourselves in the suite till we had to leave for the airport.

I rested my head against the seat back, searched my soul for self-control, and squeezed Anarchy's hand. "What if she had an affair with a married man?"

"Monica?"

I hid a smile. I wasn't the only one having trouble concentrating. "There might be a jealous wife."

"And it might be we're wasting our time, and her death is nothing more than a horrible, senseless accident."

If that were true, we could return guilt-free to the hotel.

"Monica always carried a kit. In a special monogrammed box."

He squeezed my hand. "Lily told you?"

"Yes."

"Do you think you can find out who Monica was seeing?"

"I can try."

The Almoor Country Club's clubhouse looked like Tara from *Gone with the Wind*. I half expected Vivien Leigh to rush through its graceful doors.

Instead, Ray dropped us off and pointed to a distant parking lot. "Tell them when you're ready, and they'll send a runner to get me."

"Thank you, Ray." What must he have thought as we discussed murder and cheating spouses? And the kiss. The kiss that nearly melted my resolve. The kiss that sizzled. The kiss that branded. I touched my lips—not a bit of lipstick left. I needed a stop at the powder room.

We stepped into an elegant foyer, and a woman in a black

dress smiled a welcome. "You're here for the Alexander reception?"

"Yes," Anarchy replied.

"It's in the blue room." She pointed. "Go to the end of the hall and turn right."

"Thank you." I glanced around the foyer—parquet floors, crystal chandeliers, English antiques. "You have a lovely clubhouse."

"Thank you. We're very proud of it."

Anarchy and I walked down the art-lined hallway.

I stopped and inspected a painting. "These are original and they're good."

"You sound surprised."

"I am, a little."

We heard the blue room before we saw it. A crush of people pressed around the bar and voices competed.

"Wow," Anarchy murmured.

"The best party of your life—all your friends and family—is the one you can't attend."

"It's packed."

"I get the impression she was well liked."

"Do you see Lily?"

I lifted onto my tiptoes. "No."

"You're Ellison Russell." A woman in a DVF dress clutched my arm.

I'd never seen her before, but she was looking at me as if I were her long-lost sister. "Yes."

"I can't believe it! There's something you must see." She tugged at me.

I didn't budge, and Anarchy asked, "Who are you?"

She dropped her arm and pressed her splayed fingers against her cheeks. "Oh my gracious, you must think I'm nuttier than a fruitcake. I'm Ivy Barnes."

The name meant nothing to me.

"What do you want Ellison to see?"

"Paintings. Her paintings. Three of them."

We stared at her.

"I'm making a hash of this, aren't I? We redecorated the clubhouse last year and my husband and I chaired the art committee. He picked English scenes, but I picked the art for the front hall and the ladies' lounge." She cast a meaning-laden glance at me. "Your art. I can't believe you're here."

"Go," Anarchy urged. "I'll wait in line at the bar."

I nodded.

"White wine?" he asked.

"A spritzer."

"See you in a few minutes."

Ivy led me away. "He's very handsome, your husband."

"He's not my husband."

"If I were you, I'd fix that quick." She opened a door and we walked into the ladies' lounge, where three of my paintings graced the walls. The fourth wall? Mirrors. And I definitely needed fresh lipstick.

"This is a lovely room." Soft peach, mint green, gentle florals on the matching loveseats. "I'm honored you included my work."

"Are you kidding? You're here!"

Ivy's enthusiasm was contagious, and I grinned at her.

"I had no idea you and Monica were friends. She never said a word."

Oh dear Lord. I refreshed my lipstick and searched for something less blunt than *I found her body*.

An older woman—Mother's era—entered the lounge and nodded at Ivy.

"Mrs. Waverly, nice to see you."

Mrs. Waverly inclined her chin.

"This is Ellison Russell." Ivy waved at my paintings. "The artist."

Mrs. Waverly, who smelled of Mother's perfume (Chanel No. 5), took in my suit, my pearls, and the Hermès handbag hooked over my elbow. She offered me a smile six degrees warmer than chilly. "You're the artist?"

"I am."

She stared at me for an additional ten seconds. "A pleasure to meet you."

I'd passed her silent test. "Likewise."

Ivy grinned like a lottery winner.

"If you'll excuse me, I should pay my respects." I sidled toward the door.

"Have you met David?" asked Mrs. Waverly.

"David?"

"My nephew. I believe he's reached out to your people about a gallery show."

"I've not had the pleasure."

"He's around here somewhere." Her gaze shifted to Ivy. "Perhaps you could find him."

"Sure, sure." Ivy wagged like an eager puppy.

"I look forward to meeting him before I leave." I slipped away.

Anarchy met me inside the entrance to the blue room and handed me a goblet.

"Thanks."

"Sure." He frowned. "Everything okay?"

"Fine. Have you found Lily?"

"Not yet."

"I suppose we should get in line." The queue to offer condolences snaked around the room's perimeter. "Is that—" I squinted, not believing my eyes.

"Is that who?"

"Al Winston. It is him. He's here." I nodded toward Al.

"Winston?"

"Monty went to their dinner party without Monica."

"Right."

"I took his wife to the hospital. You sat with me."

Anarchy's eyes narrowed. "And he's here? When we're married, if you're in the hospital, I won't leave your side."

Blood rushed away from my head. Not rushed—gushed. And the air—it swooshed out my lungs. I swayed.

Anarchy's quick grip on my elbow kept me from falling. "Too soon?"

Too soon? My husband wasn't dead a year. Anarchy and I had spent one night together. One. There were important things I didn't know. Did he squeeze the toothpaste from the bottom or the middle? Would he let me warm my cold feet against his legs on a chilly night? Would he find a new home for his cat? Because that animal wasn't setting foot in my house. Also, why was the room spinning?

"I'm sorry, Ellison. That just slipped out."

When we were married?

Lines etched his forehead, and his worried eyes searched my face. "Say something. Please."

He'd rendered me mute.

"Please."

"Are you asking me to marry you?" My voice was faint. I was faint.

"This—" his gaze took in the room crowded with strangers "—is not what I planned. So, no. Not here. Not at a visitation."

A tiny breath snuck into my lungs.

"But soon."

The air snuck out.

His mother. My mother. Grace. The cat. The dogs. The bright, happy flame warming my heart. Waking up to Anarchy.

Curling up on a couch to watch the late movie with Anarchy. Growing old with Anarchy.

"Tell me what you're thinking."

I forced a deep breath. "I honestly don't know."

"You love me?"

I nodded.

He exhaled. "We'll work with that."

"Ellison, what's wrong with you?" Jinx had found us.

How was I supposed to make conversation when my brain felt like a shaken snow globe? "Nothing."

She nodded at Anarchy, then asked, "Did you see Al Winston?"

A question I could answer. "Yes."

The speculative gleam in Jinx's eyes meant she was adding two and two. "I wonder..."

"Wonder what?"

She glanced at Anarchy, then held out her empty glass. "Would you mind?"

"Of course not. What are you drinking?"

"Club soda."

Anarchy's lips quirked. "Ellison, can I get you another?"

My spritzer had magically disappeared. "Club soda with a lime, please."

I watched him walk away.

"What's your plan?"

"Plan?"

"Wedding bells?"

"Jinx, stop. I'm hardly a widow."

"Tell me when you change your mind."

"Hmph. What were you wondering?"

"Al Winston's been having an affair."

"You think it was with Monica?"

"I do."

"You liked Monica."

"I did. I like loads of people who cheat on their spouses."

"You're sure?"

"Not one hundred percent. I only mention it because you've been spending so much time with Helen."

"I nearly killed her."

"Pftt." Jinx was unimpressed. "It's best to hear things like this from a friend."

"No." I held up my hands. "Not from me. First off, if they were having an affair, it's over. Second, you're not one hundred percent sure."

"Look at Al."

I glanced at where Al stood in the line to see Monty.

"He looks more upset than the husband. Positively haggard."

"Maybe he's worried about Helen. I nearly killed her."

"If he's that worried about her—" her hand made a circle in front of her non-haggard face "—why is he here? Shouldn't he be at home?"

"Monty and Al do business together. Maybe he had to come."

"You said it yourself. You nearly killed Helen. And two days later he leaves town for a funeral? Trouble with a capital T."

"You're always so suspicious."

"And I'm usually right."

There was no arguing that.

"Excuse me, I'm sorry to interrupt, but my aunt insists I introduce myself." A man with perfect hair, perfect teeth, and a perfect tan extended his hand. "I'm David Waverly. I own the gallery on State Street."

"Ellison Russell. Nice to meet you."

"Ellison—" Jinx reclaimed my attention "—George just

gave me the look. I've got to run. I'll call you when we're home. We'll talk more then." She dashed away before I could argue.

"I'm sorry, David. Jinx is a friend from home."

He nodded and flashed his perfect teeth. "I've talked with your agent."

"I heard. I'd planned on stopping by your gallery this afternoon."

"Tomorrow. Come tomorrow. I'll take you to lunch. Any favorite spots?"

"She likes the Walnut Room." Anarchy handed me my club soda and stared at David with narrowed eyes.

"David, this is Anarchy Jones. Anarchy, David Waverly. David owns the gallery I mentioned." I glanced at the drink Anarchy still held. "I'm afraid Jinx left."

David grinned. "Her husband gave her the look. When my wife gives me the look, I go running, too."

Anarchy visibly relaxed. He even took a sip of Jinx's club soda.

"Shall we stop by the gallery around eleven?"

"Perfect. You have the address?"

"I do."

"I'll look forward to seeing you. Nice meeting both of you." He dove back into the crowd.

"Can we leave?" I asked.

"You haven't talked to Lily."

"I talked to Jinx. That was more than enough."

"What did she say?"

I could hardly wait to get back to the hotel. "I'll tell you in the car."

Chapter Fourteen

We ordered breakfast from room service—eggs, croissants, bacon, and coffee (two pots).

I dressed in a simple linen shift and pretended Anarchy wasn't naked in the shower.

When the waiter knocked, I let him in and watched as he transferred covered platters from his cart to the small dining table.

"Coffee, ma'am?"

"Please. With cream."

He poured, and I took possession of the cup.

"Thank you." I signed the chit and he left me.

"That smells good." Anarchy, wrapped in a towel, leaned against the doorframe between the bedroom and living room.

My mouth went dry, and all I could manage was a croak. "Coffee?"

"I'll get it." He strode into the living room, and I reconsidered my commitment to going to Marshall Fields before we went to David's gallery.

Anarchy poured coffee into a cup, ignored the saucer, and

smirked as if he knew exactly how his still-wet chest affected me. He bent and kissed me, and my resolve wavered.

"What time are we leaving?" He was inches from me and more temptation than I could handle.

"The store opens at ten." My voice was breathy.

"It's nine thirty."

"And only one of us is dressed."

He grinned. "We could fix that."

My heart beat in my ears. "Grace gave me a list."

He sighed as if I'd wounded him, grabbed a strip of bacon, and sauntered back to the bedroom.

I clutched my coffee cup and tried not to ogle his backside.

I failed.

"Don't wait on me," he called. "Eat while it's hot."

I added eggs, bacon, and fresh berries to a plate and perused the headlines in the *Tribune*'s morning edition. Cambodians had seized an American merchant vessel, the Cubs beat the Astros, and the Daley administration was accused of patronage—all less interesting than Al Winston's affair.

Anarchy returned, kissed my cheek, and dropped into the chair next to mine.

"I've been thinking."

"About?" He looked up from helping himself to eggs. His expression said he was thinking about the Palmer House's large empty bed.

"About what Jinx said." I put down my fork, my appetite gone. "What if Helen knew? What if she did something about it?"

His gaze turned serious. "You're wondering if Helen killed Monica because she was sleeping with Al?"

I nodded.

"We don't know for certain Monica was murdered."

Monogrammed allergy kits didn't just disappear. "Helen knew about allergic reactions."

"But did she know about Monica's allergy?"

A question I couldn't answer.

Anarchy refilled his coffee cup. "Maybe Monty killed her."

"Hmph." I didn't for a second think the shell of a man I'd seen yesterday murdered his wife.

"Maybe there are additional suspects here in Chicago."

"Are you suggesting we extend our trip?"

His smile melted the polish off my toenails. "I'll stay as long as you want, but there's no proof of murder."

"Monica died at my house, then someone tried to kill me." If there was one thing I'd learned in the past year, it was that coincidences did not exist. "The two must be connected." I took a deep breath. "Also, why the secrecy? Why did she use your name?"

I stared into my empty coffee cup, and Anarchy refilled it. He was perfect that way.

"We have a woman who might have been murdered. She might have been having an affair, but the man is a mystery. And we have the attempt on your life." He scowled at that.

"I hate when things are so snarled."

"We just need to pull the right string."

"But they're all loose ends."

He leaned forward and kissed me. His lips tasted of coffee. Heaven.

I pulled away before I caved. "We have shopping to do."

"You can shop in Kansas City."

"Marshall Fields has different designers."

He sat back in his chair. "Okay."

"Okay?"

"If shopping is what makes you happy, we're going shopping."

There it was again—that bright, happy flame that told me Anarchy was right for me.

I dragged him through a down-and-dirty dash through Marshall Fields (new DVF and Missoni, a Halston pantsuit, a Gucci scarf, and a rainbow of fair isle cotton sweaters, patchwork jeans and a stack of t-shirts for Grace, and a citrusy kaftan for Aggie) and he didn't complain. Not once.

Laden with shopping bags, we arrived at David Waverly's gallery at precisely eleven.

He welcomed us with a smile that showed off his perfect teeth. "I'll show you around."

"Do you mind if I look by myself?"

He frowned but nodded.

I took a quick tour through the space. David showed pretty art with enough edge to make it interesting. His gallery and my paintings were a fit.

I returned to the two men, who stood near the gallery's entrance. "What's your timeframe, David?"

"I'd love to have you here in October."

I ticked off the finished canvases in my studio. "How many pieces?"

"At least twenty."

"A mix of mediums?"

"You're known for your acrylics."

"I've been experimenting with watercolor."

He winced. "Sure. I'd take a few watercolors." Watercolors didn't get the same respect as acrylic or oils.

I held out my hand. "I'll tell Gene." My agent would be thrilled. He'd been pushing for a Chicago show. "He'll be in touch."

"You'll do it? This is great news!"

"I look forward to it."

David glanced at his watch. "I planned on sweet-talking you for hours."

"I like your gallery."

"Thank you." He said it as if my opinion mattered. "The Berghoff for lunch?"

David took us to a restaurant with aged paneling, a decades-old patina of happy drinkers, and, framed behind the bar, Chicago's first post-Prohibition liquor license.

We settled into a comfortable booth, and the waiter served David a martini and handed out menus.

"Order a Reuben or the schnitzel." David stretched his arms across the bench on his side of the booth. "Ryan, we'll need a bottle of Champagne. We're celebrating."

Ryan made a note and took off for the bar.

"Do you mind?" David nodded at his martini.

"Please."

He took a sip. "I'm glad we met—sad it was under such unfortunate circumstances—but glad."

"How did you know Monica?" The woman was a mystery to me—a saint dedicated to helping sick kids who cheated on her husband.

"We've known each other since grade school. You?"

"I found her body."

David sprayed the table with gin.

"She came to see me and died in my late husband's study."

"She came to see you? Why?"

"No idea."

"She liked art. Maybe she was interested in your work."

If that were true, she wouldn't have given Anarchy's name. "I understand she visited Kansas City often."

"Did she?" He shrugged. "I wouldn't know. We saw each other at the club and at parties, but we weren't close."

I glanced at Anarchy and kept going. "Such an awful way to die. Monty seems bereft."

"He does seem that way." There was an edge to David's voice.

Anarchy, who held my hand under the table, tightened his grip. "He's acting?"

David shrugged. "Monica inherited a fortune from her parents. With her death, Monty Alexander became one of the richest men in Chicago."

Maybe I'd been wrong about Monty. Maybe he'd killed his wife.

THE FLIGHT to Kansas City took off too soon. Part of me wanted to stay in Chicago. In a suite at Palmer House. With Anarchy. Just the two of us. Instead, we boarded a plane and flew home.

Anarchy helped the cabbie unload my luggage, saw me to my front door, and kissed me in full view of Marian Dixon's front window.

I smiled up at him. "You just gave my neighbor heart palpitations."

"What did I do for you?" This flirty, slightly naughty side of Anarchy was wholly unexpected and entirely irresistible.

"Me? Completely unaffected." I was such a liar.

His eyes glinted as if I'd presented him with a challenge. "I have an errand. I'll be back in a couple of hours, then we'll see about those heart palpitations."

"Promise?"

He grinned and gave me a second palpitation-inducing kiss. I watched him drive away.

"You're glowing," Aggie observed from inside the front door.

Had she seen us kissing? What if she had? "Am I?"

"Definitely glowing. I'm happy for you."

The smile rising to my lips couldn't be denied.

She glanced at my left hand.

"Don't go there. I'm enjoying now."

She nodded, picked up two suitcases, and lugged them into the house. "I swear these are heavier."

"I bought a few things." I followed her with my cosmetics case and the third suitcase.

"How was the funeral?"

"Crowded. Monica was well liked." I laid the suitcase on the floor, opened it, and found the correct Marshall Fields sack. "This is for you." I held out the bag.

"For me?"

Max nudged me. I rubbed his shoulders, watched Aggie, and held my breath.

She pulled the lemony silk kaftan embroidered with silver beads from the tissue paper and stared. "It's beautiful."

"You like it?"

She stroked the fabric with her fingertips. "I love it. Thank you."

"Thank you for taking care of Grace and Max." And me. "Is she at home?"

"At Peggy's working on a project." Aggie held the kaftan to her chest. "Are you hungry? There's cold fried chicken in the fridge."

"They fed us on the plane."

She sniffed her derision. But the meal—roasted chicken, haricots verts, and whipped potatoes with chocolate brownies for dessert—hadn't been half bad.

"There are calls I need to make."

She traced the kaftan's silver embroidery. "I'll hang this up."

I settled behind my desk in the family room and dialed Libba's number. There were things I needed to share.

The answering machine picked up. I smothered my annoyance and left a perky message. "It's me. We're home. Call me."

Next I dialed Lucinda. Unlike Libba, she answered the phone. "Hello?"

"Lucinda, it's Ellison calling. How's Amy?"

"She's better. Thanks so much for asking. And thank you for the painting. It's gorgeous."

"Thank you for the flowers. Would Amy like to come to my studio?" Already the October show niggled at me—so much work to do, so much time to spend with a brush in my hand, my fingers itched with anticipation—but I'd promised a sick child.

"She'd love that. When would you like her?"

"If she's well enough, tomorrow."

"She'll be thrilled. What time?"

"Three o'clock?"

"I'll drop her off. Thanks for making time for her."

"My pleasure. See you tomorrow." I replaced the receiver.

Brnng, brnng.

"Hello?"

"You're home." Libba used her tell-me-the-whole-story tone. "Spill."

"The funeral was nice."

"Ellison." She didn't care about the funeral, and we both knew it. "Do I need to come over there?" She meant it as a threat.

"Yes."

"Are you okay?"

I was better than okay, and I was a mess. I was ebullient and terrified. I was soaring and plunging. "I—"

"Don't tell me on the phone. I'm on my way."

LIBBA CURLED in the corner of the couch and stared at me with a self-satisfied smirk. "There's only one thing that makes a woman glow like that."

"Love?"

"Fine. There are two things. Tell me everything."

I wrinkled my nose at her.

"Not the details. Broad strokes. Was it romantic? Did the earth move?" She took a sip of wine. "Of course it did—just look at you. How did it happen?"

"We went for pizza."

"You? Pizza?"

"After that, everything seemed fated."

Her eyes crinkled, and she grinned. "Oh boy, you've got it bad."

"So?" There was nothing wrong with being in love.

"You believe in soulmates."

"What if I do?" Just because Libba went through men like Kleenex didn't mean there weren't soulmates.

Her grin widened. "What will Frances say?"

"I don't care."

"Big talk. What will Harrington say?"

"He'll be glad I have a man looking out for me."

"And Grace?"

"She'll be happy for me."

She nodded. "You're right about that. She saw this coming months ago. Back to everything."

"What about it?"

"I sense there's more."

That was the problem with having the same best friend for

nearly forty years—she sensed omissions. "You're not getting details."

"Some best friend you are. Just tell me what you left out."

She'd push and prod and wheedle till I told her. And I *wanted* to tell someone. "We were at the visitation and—"

"And you did it in a closet! Ellison Russell, I didn't know you had that in you." Her grin was maniacal.

"We did not have sex in a closet."

"Don't be judgy. And don't knock it till you try it."

I held up my hands. "Not another word."

"Fine." She rolled her eyes. "What happened at the visitation?"

"Anarchy said..." How to explain?

Long seconds passed.

"Are you making me guess?" she demanded.

"No." I swallowed a gulp of wine. "We were talking about being in the hospital, and Anarchy said when we were married he'd—"

"What?" Libba screeched.

In the kitchen, Max howled.

"Was this before or after?"

"After."

Libba put her wine on the coffee table and gave her hands a gleeful rub. "That man went from zero to sixty fast. What did you say?"

"I was too shocked to say anything. Then he said it wasn't a proposal. Yet."

"Do you want to get married?"

"My first marriage was a disaster."

"This time you found the right man."

"I thought that with Henry."

"You were wrong. I remember telling you not to rush into anything. But, no—you wouldn't listen. Now? Rush!"

"There are things to consider."

"What will Frances say?"

"I repeat, I don't care. I'm more worried about Celeste."

"You told me she went back to California. Frances is the threat. She's here. And she's ready, willing, and able to meddle in your life. Have you talked about children?"

"Children?" My stomach dropped.

"Does Anarchy want any?"

"I'm too old."

"No. You're not."

Grace was almost out of the house. And, as much as I'd adored raising her, I didn't want to spend the next years feeding a baby or changing diapers, staying up till midnight to finish a sugar cube diorama, or policing parties.

I deflated. "What if he wants kids?"

"Ask him."

"What if he says yes?"

"Then talk about it."

"You make it sound easy."

"It is."

"If it's so easy, why aren't you married?"

"I don't believe in soulmates. I'm fickle. I change my mind the way I change my shoes." She shifted her gaze to her wedge sandals. "Today's Mr. Right is tomorrow's Mr. Boring." She frowned and crossed her legs. "We're not talking about me." She clapped. "This is so exciting! I haven't been in a wedding in years."

"Libba—"

"I'm your maid of honor." Her expression dared me to argue. "Big wedding?"

"No!"

"Why not?"

"I've already had one."

"Anarchy hasn't. Where is he?"

"He said he had an errand."

Her answering grin made the Cheshire Cat seem like a sourpuss. "He went to see your father."

"What? No. I'm a widow. I don't need my father's permission."

"True. I bet Anarchy is asking for his blessing."

This was too fast. I shook my head.

"Ellison, the man follows the rules. It's who he is. Did you really think he'd take you to bed and not put a ring on your finger?"

"Ellison Walford Russell!" Mother's outraged voice echoed through the house.

Libba giggled. "Sounds like Frances knows. Are you sure you don't care what she thinks?"

Chapter Fifteen

Amy Sandhurst clutched my hand as we climbed the stairs to my studio. Back when Henry considered my art an amusing hobby, he'd paid to convert the third-floor ballroom to my dream atelier. We'd added skylights, expanded windows, and created a light-filled oasis.

Amy gasped when we reached the top of the steps.

An enormous table sat in the room's center. Stacks of books on art and architecture, jars of paintbrushes, boxes of pastels, and an assortment of pencils and drawing pads covered half its surface. Near the room's south windows, two squashy armchairs invited daydreaming. The smell of turpentine, graphite pencils, and gum erasers was as familiar and comfortable as favorite slippers. I breathed deep and felt a smile settle on my lips.

Amy let go of my hand and approached the easel I'd adjusted for her height. With hesitant fingers she touched the wood. "For me?"

"Mhmm. What would you like to paint?"

Her face clouded. "I don't know."

"You'll figure it out. Do you want watercolors or acrylics? Those are types of paint."

"The painting you did for Mommy?"

"Watercolor."

"That's what I want."

"We sit down for that." I tore a blank sheet of watercolor paper from a pad and clipped it to a board. Together, we perched on stools at the table's uncluttered end, and I opened a box of watercolors and showed her how to mix colors. "Blue and yellow for green. Blue and red for purple. Red and yellow make orange."

"Pink?"

"Red and white. Maybe a little blue." I showed her how to deepen hues and balance brightness. "Are you ready?"

She nodded.

"There's one important thing to remember."

"What?" Her voice was breathless and her eyes enormous.

"Art should be fun. There are no mistakes. If you don't like how something turns out, try again."

She frowned. "Isn't that a mistake?"

"No. It's a lesson. It's how we learn."

Amy nodded, her face serious—as if I were imparting the wisdom of the ages. "What about gray?"

"Mix black and white. Sometimes I draw a quick sketch before I paint. Then I color in the lines."

"Could I paint my family?"

"Whatever you want. Do you want my help sketching?"

"No thank you. I can do it."

"Okay. Let me know if you need anything." I dug through my books, found one about Chicago, and studied a photo of Oak Street Beach taken from the water. The Gold Coast's building stretched skyward in the background.

With the largest piece of watercolor paper I had clipped to a board, I sat kitty-corner from Amy.

The brush in my hand was an old friend. Together, we painted. I chose turquoise for Lake Michigan. I let the sunlight gild the city. Cherubic children dug in the sand.

The colors were happy.

The children were happy—a boy digging in the sand, a laughing girl running with her hair and sundress streaming behind her.

Their mother was happy.

The puffy pink clouds in a lemon-hued sky were happy.

The boy's red sand bucket was happy.

The—I frowned and blotted the boy's head.

"Did you make a mistake?" asked Amy.

"No mistakes. Remember?"

"Not even for grownups?"

A loaded question. "When it comes to art? No mistakes."

When it came to life? Another story.

Mother had made a mistake when she barged into my house and told me I was thinking with Celeste's favorite anatomical part.

Had I made a mistake when I rose from the couch with stiff arms and fisted hands?

"He's marrying you for your money."

"Get out."

She'd gaped at me.

"Get out of my house."

"I'm your mother."

"That does not give you the right to speak to me that way. Get out of my house."

I could have explained I loved him. I could have told her he had more money than Midas. But I'd kicked her out.

Mistake?

Libba's dumbstruck expression and my own shaking knees told me I'd crossed a line.

In that moment, with rage and hurt coursing through me, I hadn't cared.

Today? Today I preferred to think about Anarchy and the best shade for the John Hancock Building.

Amy and I painted in silence.

"May I have another piece of paper?"

I looked up from the sun-kissed children on the beach. "Of course. Would you like me to wash your brushes?"

She nodded, and I collected the brushes she'd used. The water from the sink in the corner turned black when it hit the soft bristles. Whatever Amy had painted was dark.

Poor kid. She lived with illness.

"Amy?"

"Yes, Mrs. Russell?"

"What makes you happy?"

"School."

"What else?"

"Cake."

Cake I could work with. "May I show you something?"

She nodded.

I sifted through my books till I found one that included Wayne Thiebaud's paintings—a slice of cherry pie, cakes, gumball machines. "Look at this." I held the open book out to Amy.

She stared, transfixed. "There are no people."

"No."

"No flowers. No houses."

"No."

"Can I do that?"

"Of course."

Together we sketched a slice of cake, then Amy painted—Amy *smiled* and painted.

I returned to the troublesome boy on the beach. His hair was too blond. Sun-kissed brown was better.

We painted in companionable silence till Aggie's voice came through the intercom. "Mrs. Sandhurst is here."

I glanced at my watch and frowned. "She's early." Lucinda wasn't due for another thirty minutes. I crossed to the box on the wall and pushed the button. "Please offer her coffee. We'll be down in a few minutes." I released the button and turned to Amy. "Are you done?"

Her forehead puckered. "She came too soon."

"If you'd like, you can leave your painting and finish another day."

She squinted at her paper. "No. I think I'm done."

"Do you like it?"

She offered me a shy smile and nodded.

"May I see it?"

She turned the board.

Amy's cake was pink and blue and yellow.

"That looks delicious. You're very talented."

Her cheeks flushed. "Thank you."

"Shall we take it downstairs?"

"Yes, please."

I held her painting flat, and we descended the steps.

Lucinda (who'd inexplicably declined coffee) waited in the foyer. "Did you have a nice time?"

Amy nodded.

"What do you say?"

"Thank you for having me to your studio, Mrs. Russell."

"I'm so glad you came. Would you like to come again?"

Her face lit up. "Can I?"

I glanced at Lucinda, a question in my eyes.

She gave me a small nod.

"Of course you may."

"Thank you, Ellison."

"You're welcome. She's a joy."

The front door opened, and Anarchy stepped inside.

Lucinda's brows rose in that-man-entered-your-house-without-knocking surprise.

"Have you two met?"

"I don't believe so." Anarchy extended his hand. "Anarchy Jones."

"Lucinda Jones—" her cheeks colored "—I mean, Lucinda Sandhurst. Nice to meet you."

Anarchy pretended he didn't notice her slip and shifted his gaze to the little girl half-hiding behind her mother. "Hi. I'm Anarchy."

"That's a funny name."

"Amy!" Lucinda's voice was severe.

"No. She's right. I've never met anyone else with my name."

"There are three Amys in my class."

"That must get confusing."

Amy scowled at her mother. "I guess. I miss a lot of school."

"You came to paint with Ellison?"

Amy nodded.

"May I see your painting?"

She nodded.

Anarchy studied the paper and grinned. "That makes me hungry for cake. Ellison, let's have cake for dinner."

Amy giggled.

Lucinda took hold of Amy's hand. "We need to get going, sweetie. Your father promised he'd be home for dinner."

Amy's lips pursed, and she gazed longingly at the stairs.

"Same time next week?"

Amy's smile was brighter than sunshine. "Please, Mommy?"

"We'll see how you're feeling."

They left us, and Anarchy wrapped his arms around me. "Hi."

"Hi."

He dipped his head for a kiss.

After a blissful moment, I pulled away. "I should clean up the studio. Do you want to grab a couple of glasses of wine and join me?"

"I thought the studio was off limits."

"By invitation only."

"And I'm invited?"

"Definitely." I brushed a kiss against his cheek and climbed the stairs. Straightening the table and cleaning the brushes took only a moment. When I turned away from the sink, Anarchy stood behind me.

I took a glass of wine from his hand. "Thank you."

"This is amazing." He cast his gaze around the studio.

"I like it."

He walked over to the table and looked down at my beach scene. "You started this today?"

"This afternoon."

"You're amazing." He settled onto a stool, pulled Amy's forgotten painting toward him, and frowned. "She's the sick girl?" He'd been marvelous with her.

"We should talk."

"Uh-oh."

"You're good with children."

He frowned as if I wasn't making sense.

"Do you want your own?"

"Do you want more?"

"No." My answer was definitive. I was almost forty. I didn't want to start over.

He sagged as if relieved by my answer. "Neither do I."

"You're giving up your chance to—"

"No. I'm not. I like kids. Especially Grace. But I never considered having my own. It's never been a goal."

Was he just saying that? Would he resent me in five years when it was too late? "You're sure?"

"Positive."

He glanced again at Amy's painting, and I looked over his shoulder.

She'd painted her family in moody purples, funereal black, and drab blue. Her brothers were light gray. The little girl in the painting was wispy—as if she might fade off the page.

"I wish there was more I could do for her."

"That cake was a happier picture."

I kissed the back of his ear. "It was, wasn't it?"

He swiveled the stool, turning to face me. "I didn't expect you to ask me about kids."

"What did you expect?"

"I caused a problem between you and your mother."

"SHE EAVESDROPPED." Not that she'd admit that. In her mind, when her daughter's beau showed up unannounced and asked to speak to her husband, she was entitled to hear what he said. "Mother and I will work things out." I'd forgive her. Eventually. Whether she forgave Daddy for giving Anarchy his blessing was a separate issue. "Have you told your mother?"

"You haven't officially said yes."

"You haven't officially asked."

He gathered me into his arms and kissed the corner of my mouth.

"Her reaction might make Mother's look mild."

"Let's forget our mothers." He pulled me closer.

The part of my brain wired for worry fritzed. "Deal."

"I'm sorry to interrupt—" Aggie's voice came from the intercom "—but Helen Winston is on the phone."

"I should take that."

Anarchy loosened his hold. "Because you think she's responsible for Monica Alexander's death?"

"That, and I almost killed her." I crossed to the intercom. "I'll plug in the phone."

I put the cord in the jack and picked up the receiver. "Hello, Helen."

In the kitchen, Aggie hung up her line.

"Ellison, I'm calling to thank you for the flowers. They're magnificent."

I'd sent a bouquet before I left for Chicago. "I'm so glad you like them. How are you feeling?"

"One hundred percent better."

"It's too bad you couldn't go to the funeral with Al." The subtle part of my brain was fritzed as well.

"Monica Alexander's? I barely knew her."

"I saw Al there."

"Did you? He didn't say. Monty sits on the board of one of Al's companies."

"Her death was such a tragedy. I can't tell you how grateful I am you had your allergy kit handy."

"Bees. Nuts. They're everywhere. Not to speak ill of the dead, but it was irresponsible of her not to carry a kit."

"It's such a mystery. Her friends swear she never left home without it."

"Are you suggesting someone took her kit? Why would someone do that?"

"There's some speculation she was having an affair."

Helen was silent for long seconds. "You can't think Monty took her kit. The man is a giant teddy bear."

"Monty. Or maybe the man's wife."

"What are you saying, Ellison? You can't think Liz had anything to do with this."

"Liz?"

"Liz Burkhart. Monica and Randal were having an affair. I thought you knew."

Now, I was silent.

"It can't matter," Helen continued. "Even if Liz did take the kit, Monica died from a bee sting. She's not responsible for that. Listen, the oven just dinged. I've got to run. Thank you again for the flowers."

I stared at the dead receiver.

"What's wrong?"

"According to Helen, Monica was having an affair with Randal Burkhart."

"Do you think she's right?"

"Liz mentioned trouble, but not that."

"Would she?"

"You'd be surprised how many women confide in me. Maybe because Henry cheated in such spectacular fashion. His exploits make their husbands' transgressions look mild."

Anarchy rose from the stool and wrapped me in his arms. "You can depend on me."

Maybe there would come a day when being in Anarchy's arms didn't weaken my knees, but I doubted it.

"Forever." He pulled me closer.

"Dinner will be ready in ten minutes." Aggie's voice boomed from the intercom, and we both jumped.

"What did she fix?" he asked.

"Not cake."

Chapter Sixteen

"What are you doing today?" A ready-for-the-day Anarchy smiled at me across the kitchen island. That smile curled his lips, softened his cheeks, and sparkled in his eyes.

That smile curled my toes, softened my knees, and sparkled in my veins. I smiled back and smoothed the front of my bathrobe. "I thought I'd take the painting Amy forgot to the Sandhursts' house."

He raised his brows and refrained from telling me to mind my own business.

"She might need a psychologist." That poor child. "What about you? What are you doing today?"

"I've had uniforms canvasing auto-body repair shops. There are a few leads." He studied my expression, and added, "Don't get your hopes up. There are a couple cars with front right fender damage. Nothing may come of it."

"Take your time finding that car."

"What?"

"I like having you here."

"I like being here." He joined me on the Mr. Coffee-side of

the island and reached into his pocket. "We could make this permanent. Ellison, would—"

Clop, clop, clop.

"She's not sneaking up on anyone in those shoes." Anarchy took his hand from his pocket.

My heart, which had been jack-rabbiting around my chest, calmed enough for me to pour my second (much-needed) cup of coffee.

Grace burst into the kitchen. "Good morning." She spotted Aggie's muffins on the island. "Score!" She grabbed one, then wagged a finger at me. "Don't give this batch away."

"We haven't caused Margaret any trouble—" I cast my gaze on Max "—lately."

Grace crouched next to the still-mopey dog and scratched behind his ears. "Pansy will be home soon. Promise."

He whined and thumped his stubby tail.

Grace stood. "I'm going to Peggy's after school. We're almost done with our project."

"What are you working on?" Anarchy asked.

"An oral history project. We interviewed women who were born before women had the right to vote about how voting has affected women's lives."

"What did you conclude?"

"A lot more change needs to happen." She crammed half a muffin in her mouth and walked to the back door. "See you later."

"Will you be home for dinner?" I called after her.

"Don't count on me."

Max rose from his corner, shook his ears, then hoovered the trail of crumbs Grace left behind.

"May I take you to dinner tonight?"

A restaurant? Where neither Aggie nor Grace nor even Mother could interrupt us? "I'd like that."

He gave me a quick kiss. "It's a date. Six o'clock?"

I nodded, watched him leave, and sighed.

You like him, don't you? If you like him, I like him. Any other man would be jealous. Not Mr. Coffee.

"I love him," I whispered.

As long as you're happy.

"I am." I floated upstairs and threw on a sunny yellow and pink Lilly shift with matching pink sandals. Then I fetched Amy's painting and the book with Wayne Thiebaud's paintings from the studio and drove to the Sandhursts'.

The doorbell echoed. Should I have called first? Were they home?

The front door swung open, and a woman in a maid's uniform gave me a polite smile.

"Is Mrs. Sandhurst home?"

"No, ma'am."

"Amy came to my house yesterday to paint. She left one of her paintings. May I—"

"Miss Amy is here."

"She is?" It was a school day.

"I keep an eye on her when Mrs. Sandhurst has a hair or nail appointment."

"I see." I didn't.

"Would you like to give the painting to Amy?"

"I have a book for Amy."

"Please, come in."

I followed her up the front stairs.

She paused halfway down the hallway, knocked, then opened a door. "You have a visitor."

"Good morning." I stepped into Amy's room. She and Oliver curled amongst a mound of pillows in a four-poster bed with a pink gingham canopy. A coordinating spread covered the bed. Valances of the same fabric topped the windows.

Beneath my feet, the shag carpet was also pink. "How are you feeling?"

She looked frail and tired but offered me a weak smile. "I'm okay. Just tired."

"I'll let you visit." The housekeeper disappeared.

"I brought you the book with the Wayne Thiebaud paintings. I thought you might want to look through it."

"Thank you."

I sat the book in her lap.

She stroked the cover with shaking hands, then opened to the first page. "Ouch!" She stuck her finger in her mouth.

"Did you cut yourself?"

She nodded.

"Paper cuts are the worst. Do you need a Band-Aid?"

She eyed her finger. "Yes, please."

"Where's the bathroom?"

"That way." She pointed to a closed door.

I entered the pink and white bathroom and opened the medicine cabinet. Not surprisingly, it was filled with prescriptions. I shoved them aside looking for Band-Aids and antiseptic cream and knocked an apothecary bottle to the floor.

Fortunately, it didn't break.

I bent, picked up the bottle, and recognized the label from a holistic store in Westport.

Hmm. As sick as Amy was, Lucinda shouldn't be giving her unprescribed herbs. What did this stuff do? I memorized the label and returned to Amy's bedroom. "Let's see that finger."

She held out her hand. Had Grace ever been so thin?

I dabbed cream and wrapped a Band-Aid around her bony finger. "Better?"

She nodded. "Yes. Thank you."

"Shall we look at the book together?"

"I'd like that. You could tell me about the other artists." She made room for me on the bed.

Together we looked at photographs of paintings by Jasper Johns, Jackson Pollock, Mark Rothko, Willem de Kooning, Roy Lichtenstein, and Andy Warhol. Wayne Thiebaud remained her favorite. She returned again and again to his cake paintings.

When she yawned, I slid off the bed. "You should rest."

"I'm not tired." Amy sounded like every child who'd ever fought sleep.

"I can tell. Will you take care of my book till I see you next week?"

Her eyes grew wide. "I can borrow it?"

"Of course you may."

She hugged the book to her chest, and I considered calling Wayne Thiebaud. He'd moved away from painting pastries, but perhaps he'd make an exception for a sick child.

"Thank you, Mrs. Russell."

"You're welcome." I dropped a quick kiss on her head. "Now get some rest."

With her arms still wrapped around the book, Amy closed her eyes.

The need to do something scratched at me. Rather than go home, I drove to Westport. In the market for Birkenstocks, hemp clothing, or batik pillows? They were available in Westport.

Since I'd never been in the market for any of those things, I had to search for the apothecary. I found it tucked between a vintage clothing shop and a used bookstore. When I entered, the scent of patchouli smacked me in the face.

The young woman behind the counter wore a long gypsy dress and granny glasses. Shaggy locks surrounded her face.

From the time Marjorie and I were old enough to pick out our own clothes, Mother had insisted that skirts and blouses, shoes and handbags, dresses and scarves mattered. Clothes helped form first impressions. They told a story. They made a statement.

The woman's bohemian clothes told me she believed in the stuff she sold. Her clothes said she enjoyed the smell of patchouli. Her clothes said she drank carrot juice for breakfast and ate alfalfa sprouts for lunch.

"How may I help you?"

"I'm interested in apitoxin."

Her smile was sympathetic. "For arthritis?"

Arthritis? That couldn't be right. Whatever Amy had, it wasn't arthritis.

My face must have registered surprise, because she asked, "You're sure that's what you want?"

"I think so. May I please see the bottle?"

She turned to the shelf behind her and selected a bottle identical to the one I'd dropped. "How did you hear about it?"

"A friend."

"Most of our business comes from referrals."

I took the bottle. "What's the science behind it?"

"It's actually an ancient remedy. People have been using it for thousands of years to ease arthritis pain."

"How does it work?"

"It reduces inflammation."

Did Lucinda think Amy suffered from some kind of inflammation? Did her doctors know about the apitoxin? Drugs could interact. Easily a quarter of my friends were married to doctors; I could ask one of them. If it was harmless, Lucinda need never know I'd stuck my nose in. "How much is it?"

"Four hundred."

I nearly dropped the bottle. "Dollars?" Four hundred dollars would pay for several nights in the suite at the Palmer

House, two weeks of Aggie's salary, or a color television. "What makes it so expensive?"

The woman took in my Lilly shift, my pink sandals, the leather handbag slung over my shoulder, and the Wayfarer sunglasses I'd pushed into my hair when I entered the dim shop. What did my clothes say about me? At the club, I'd fit in. But here—in Westport—they said I was a spoiled wife who didn't want to spend this month's clothing budget on a little brown bottle.

"The ingredients are expensive, but they work." Her eyes widened with sincerity. "Apitoxin changes lives. People with hands curled by pain can grip a pen again. People with bad knees can walk again."

Very nice. But what did that have to do with Amy? "How is it used?"

"A drop every morning."

"Side effects?"

She frowned. "A few people develop a skin rash. Does it work for your friend?"

The shop's door jangled open and the young woman's gaze shifted. "Would you excuse me for a moment?" She didn't wait for my answer. "I have your order ready, Mrs. Smith."

While she rang up the new customer's order, I perused the shelves. In addition to apothecary bottles filled with dubious elixirs, the shop sold essential oils, Ben Wa balls in silk boxes, self-help books, and vegan cookbooks.

When Mrs. Smith completed her purchase, I drifted back to the counter. "Is a rash the only side effect?"

"A few people develop stomach aches."

"What? How many?"

"It's wonderful for arthritis—"

"How many?"

"Twenty-five to thirty percent."

"What is this stuff?"

"What do you mean?"

"You said the ingredients are expensive. What are they?"

"You don't know?"

I gave her Mother's gorgon gaze, and she took a step backward.

"If I knew, I wouldn't ask."

"It's venom."

"Snake venom?"

"No. Bee venom."

The world around me slowed, and I gripped the counter's edge. "Bee venom?"

She nodded. "We have exclusive selling rights for the area."

I held up a hand. "Bee venom?"

"Yes." Her tone said she was tired of the question. "It's for arthritis."

"How much do you sell?"

"It's expensive."

It was very expensive. "How much do you sell?"

"We have dedicated customers."

"I need a list."

"What? No."

I refused to argue with her. "May I use your telephone?"

"It's not available for the public."

"Fine." I stalked out and race-walked down the street to The Prospect, the one place I knew in Westport. The Prospect served a fabulous steak soup, a delicious Caesar salad, and miniature loaves of fresh bread baked in flowerpots.

"Mrs. Russell, how nice to see you," said the hostess. "Just one today?"

I nodded. "Before you seat me, may I use the phone?"

"Of course. There's a payphone just outside the ladies'

room—" She blanched as I borrowed Mother's fiercest expression. "Let me take you to the office."

"Thank you." I followed her to the manager's tidy office, waited till she left, and called Anarchy.

"Detective Jones' office."

"This is Ellison Russell calling. I have an emergency. Would you please have him call me at—" I read the number from the center of the phone's rotary dial.

"Yes, Mrs. Russell."

A minute later the phone rang, and I grabbed the receiver. "Hello."

"Ellison? What happened? Are you okay?"

"I'm fine. Did you know it's possible to buy bee venom?"

His answering silence made me wonder if I'd made a mistake calling this an emergency.

"You gave me a heart attack."

"I'm sorry. There's one place in all of Kansas City that sells bee venom."

"Where are you?"

"The Prospect in Westport."

"Stay there. I'm on my way."

I returned to the hostess stand, thanked her, and followed her to a table, where a waiter took my order.

The waiter delivered my soup as Anarchy arrived.

"You ordered lunch?"

"They let me use their phone, I had to order something."

His lips quirked, and he sat across from me.

"Are you hungry?" I pushed the bowl across the table.

"No." He pushed it back. "Tell me about the bee venom."

I told him about the bottle at the Sandhursts', how the label read apitoxin, and how the Stevie Nicks wannabe said apitoxin was bee venom.

"Why do the Sandhursts have it?" he asked.

"Maybe Bill has arthritis. We need to get that shop's customer list."

He raised his brows.

"What if Helen or Liz are on it?"

Anarchy walked me to my car and sent me home. "Go." He kissed my forehead. "We'll figure out who owns the store, and, if necessary, we can get a warrant for their customer files."

I nodded but didn't move.

"I didn't believe Monica was murdered, but you found the murder weapon and the killer's trail." Another kiss—this one on the lips. "I'll see you at six."

"But the case—"

"Nothing—and I do mean nothing—will keep me from taking you to dinner tonight."

My heart did a little shimmy.

When I arrived home, a harried Aggie met me at the front door. "Your mother has called eight times."

Brnng, brnng.

"I'll give you hazard pay if you tell her I'm not home."

Aggie shook her head. "Your neighbor probably called her the second you pulled into the driveway."

I turned, looked across the street, and caught the glint of Marian Dixon's binoculars.

Brnng, brnng.

With leaden feet, I walked into the study and picked up the receiver. "Hello."

"We need to talk."

"No, Mother. We don't."

"Don't be unreasonable."

"Me? I think unreasonable is telling me I'm thinking with my vagina." I could almost see her cringe at my use of Celeste's favorite word. "I think unreasonable is suggesting the man I love only cares about my money."

"I was rash."

Rash? She'd been utterly horrible, and rather than apologize she'd called me unreasonable.

"Say something," she demanded.

"I have nothing to say to you."

"I want what's best for you."

"No. You want what's best for you." Marjorie had married a condom manufacturer. Mother wanted me married to a doctor or lawyer or business owner. Instead, I chose a cop.

Her enemies might snicker.

Her friends might snicker.

I said a silent prayer—*Please, God, let me never do this to Grace. Let her be her own woman. Give me the strength to let her go.*

"Ellison, are you there?"

"Yes, Mother."

"Did you hear me?"

"I'm afraid not." I'd been busy praying.

"I said I'm sorry."

"Sorry?" Mother never apologized. It gave her indigestion.

"If you'd told me his family's history, we wouldn't have had this problem."

Again, my fault. I ground my teeth and—wait. "How do you know about his family?"

"I've got to run, dear. I look forward to planning the wedding."

Chapter Seventeen

I hung up the phone and collapsed into the nearest chair. How had Mother found out about Anarchy's family? Gossiping friends from San Francisco? More likely she'd hired a private investigator to dig up reasons I shouldn't be with him. I bet his background had come as a huge surprise.

Why did she imagine I'd let her plan my wedding?

I closed my eyes and anticipated battles over the guest list, the dress, the food, the flowers, and the wording on the invitations.

"Are you okay?" Aggie peeked through the doorway.

"I need a drink."

"Coffee?"

"Or something stronger." I glanced at my watch. A quarter till two was definitely too early to crack a bottle. "Do we have any pie?"

"There's chocolate cake."

I sighed. "It will have to do."

We shuffled (I shuffled) to the kitchen, and Aggie sat me down on a stool and served me coffee.

I wrapped my hands around the filled-to-the-brim goodness and watched her cut an enormous slice of cake. She put it on a plate, added vanilla ice cream, and positioned it in front of me.

"He hasn't asked me yet."

"Pardon?"

"Libba volunteered to be my maid of honor, and Mother says she's planning the wedding, but he hasn't asked me."

"He will."

Why did things have to be so difficult? I ate a bite of cake and moaned. "This is marvelous."

"Thank you. It's a new recipe." She wiped her hands on a tea towel. "There are few more messages from this morning."

I shoveled in another bite. "Who?"

"Jinx, Libba, and Mrs. Burkhart."

"Liz? What did she want?"

"She didn't say. She just asked that you call her."

"Jinx told me Monica Alexander was having an affair with Al Winston, but Helen told me Monica was seeing Randal Burkhart."

"Who do you believe?"

I rubbed my hands across my face. "Jinx is seldom wrong."

"I sense a 'but.'"

"Al Winston isn't the sort of man to put a business relationship at risk for a woman."

Brnng, brnng.

I scowled at the phone.

Aggie picked up the receiver. "Russell residence." Five seconds passed. "I'm sorry, she went to her studio and asked not to be disturbed." A full minute passed before she said, "I'll give her the message."

She hung up the phone but didn't turn.

"Aggie, who was that?"

"Your mother."

"What did she want?"

"She's arranged meetings with three different florists next Thursday. Your first appointment is at one."

"He hasn't asked. I haven't said yes."

Aggie regarded me with sympathy-filled eyes. "You were telling me about Mrs. Burkhart."

"Right." Far better to think about murder than Mother's plans for my wedding. "If it's true, if Monica and Randal were having an affair, Liz had a motive."

"How did she plan a bee sting?"

I told her about apitoxin.

"She might have had motive and means, but did she have the opportunity?"

Brnng, brnng.

We both stared at the phone.

"We could let the machine pick up," I suggested.

Aggie smoothed her kaftan—purple with turquoise flowers —over her hips. "If it's her, she knows we're home."

"Starting tomorrow, we're killing Marian Dixon with kindness. Cakes, muffins, pies—whatever it takes to turn her to our side." Mother having a spy across the street was intolerable.

Aggie nodded and picked up the phone. "Russell residence —yes, she's still in the studio—"

Oh dear Lord. What now?

"Yes, I'm writing this down." She wasn't. "I'll give her the message."

"What? What now?" I asked as Aggie hung up the receiver.

"You have appointments with cake ladies on Friday afternoon."

I didn't want a stranger making my cake. "I was hoping you'd do that for us. Would you? Please?"

"He hasn't asked you yet. And I'd be honored."

Brnng, brnng.

I stood. "I'm going to the studio."

Aggie grinned. "I'm happy for you. You deserve a man who loves you the way he does."

My eyes filled with tears. "Thank you." I hurried up the back stairs, away from whatever Mother had planned with the bridal shops.

In the studio, I threw a smock over my dress and settled a primed canvas on an easel.

Aggie had brought Lucinda's peonies upstairs, and they sat on the table fully bloomed. A few petals rested on the table's surface. They were beautiful.

I angled the easel and squeezed paints onto a pallet.

I wanted delicate pinks, but my paintbrush had other ideas. The pinks turned dark, bordering on pure phthalo blue. The fallen petals looked like blackened bones.

I stepped back and sighed in frustration. The painting wasn't bad, but it wasn't what I had planned.

Almost nothing was.

I glanced at the phone. Should I plug it in and call Liz?

And say what?

Asking if she'd murdered her husband's mistress might set a confrontational tone.

I was so *tired* of murder.

And you're marrying a homicide detective? asked a voice in my head (the voice sounded a lot like Mother's).

"He hasn't asked me," I snapped.

Having an argument with a voice in my head bordered on crazy.

I cleaned my brushes. The peony painting was too dark, and I wasn't in the right mood to paint. Instead, I flung myself into an armchair and tucked my feet beneath me.

What had Aggie said? Motive, means, and opportunity.

No one had all three.

At least that I knew of.

I hauled myself out of the chair, plugged in the phone, and called Jinx. "What time did the luncheon at Lucinda's end?"

"Hello to you, too."

"Just answer the question."

"Why?"

"What time, Jinx?"

"I'd guess around half-past one." That meant only thirty minutes passed between the luncheon's end and her arrival at my house. Who could she have met?

"Best wishes," said Jinx.

"Best wishes?"

"I hear you're getting married."

"He. Hasn't. Asked. Me." I pinched the bridge of my nose. "How do you know?"

"Karen Park saw him at Tivol's." The Plaza jewelry store was where I took my pearls to be restrung, where Henry bought my jewelry, and where brides picked their engagement rings. "Apparently he was having the prongs put on an heirloom set. Karen saw the ring. She says it's stunning. Three karats and—"

"Jinx!"

"What?"

"With love, shut the hell up."

"You want it to be a surprise?"

"Yes."

"Sorry. Drat! Listen, the yard man is here. May I call you later?"

"If you promise not to tell me about the ring."

"You're sure? Karen said it—"

"Stop!"

"Fine," she huffed. "Talk to you later."

Rather than return to my seat by the window, I picked up the Oak Street Beach watercolor.

Painted when I was bursting with happiness, the whole scene was joyous—the laughing children, their smiling mother, the sky, even the skyline. The edges were sharp. I cut my finger. "Ouch." I stuck my injured finger in my mouth.

And I knew.

I yanked off the smock and careened down the stairs. "Aggie!"

She didn't answer.

I looked out a back window.

Her VW Bug wasn't in its usual spot.

I grabbed the phone and dialed Anarchy's number.

"Detective Jones' office."

"This is Ellison Russell."

"Another emergency?" The voice was wry.

"Yes! Please tell him to meet me at the Sandhursts'." I hung up the phone and raced to my car.

The same uniformed maid answered the Sandhursts' door.

"Good afternoon." Somehow I kept my voice even. "Is Mrs. Sandhurst home?"

"No, ma'am."

"What about Amy?"

She nodded but didn't move.

"May I see her?"

She hesitated.

"I loaned her a book and I'm afraid I need it back."

She stood aside.

I brushed past her. "I know the way."

Amy looked tiny. Her eyes fluttered open when I entered her room.

"How are you feeling?"

"My tummy hurts today."

"Amy." I sat on the edge of the bed. "Does the medicine your mommy gives you make your stomach hurt?"

She pulled the sheets higher on her chest and stared at me with enormous eyes. "Mommy loves me."

"Of course she does."

Amy's eyes filled with tears. "I get so mad. I want to go to school."

I held my breath.

"But we can't let Daddy forget us."

I closed my eyes so she wouldn't see the horror in them.

"You're very brave to tell me. Did you tell anyone else?"

"Mommy says it's our secret and if I tell, Daddy will go away, but—" her chin quivered "—the nice lady asked me. She said she could make Mommy stop."

"Amy!" Lucinda stood in the doorway.

Amy shrank to Oliver's size.

I stood. "How could you?"

"I had to." She took a breath and pressed her right hand against her chest. "Bill stopped seeing me. I gave him every-thing—my youth, a second family, my love—and he can't be bothered to act like a husband or father. The man works and plays golf with his cronies."

What she'd done was so twisted, so wrong, I simply gaped at her.

"Last winter, Amy got pneumonia. Bill cancelled a golf trip and he told me I was an angel, the way I took care of her."

"Why Amy?"

"Bill doesn't care if the boys get sick. He expects them to tough it out. But he worries about his daughter."

"Lucinda..." What did one say to a crazy woman?

"Don't judge me. You have no idea what it's like when your husband doesn't see you."

Actually, I knew exactly what it was like. And never, in a

million, trillion years, would I have hurt Grace to gain his attention. "What about Monica?"

"Amy told her. I knew she'd interfere, so I followed her to your house."

My stomach roiled. "How?"

"I dipped a safety pin in apitoxin and stopped her in your driveway."

"You scratched her."

"There was nothing I could do to change her mind. I had to stop her."

"Mommy?"

"Be quiet, Amy."

"What now?" I didn't like the way Lucinda looked at us. Where was Anarchy?

She lifted her left hand from the folds of her skirt and pointed a .22 at me.

Amy sobbed.

"You won't shoot me."

"Don't bet on that." She released the safety.

I put up my hands. "Please. Not in front of Amy."

"None of this would have happened if she'd kept quiet."

Amy's face was blotchy, and her eyes swollen. "I'm sorry, Mommy."

"Quiet!" She stepped away from the door and gestured me through it. "Go."

"Which way?"

"Toward the stairs."

She followed a few steps behind me. I had to stop her. When she was done with me, she'd hurt Amy. I was sure of it.

"Lucinda..."

"Go." The gun in my back had me descending the first step.

I resisted taking a second step. "Bernie!"

"I sent her to the market."

Right. Bernie was buying milk and eggs and bread while Lucinda murdered me.

The pressure on my back increased. "Go."

What could I do? How could I save us?

The pressure from the gun disappeared, and I dared a glance over my shoulder. Behind me, Lucinda's arms windmilled as she tried to maintain her balance.

Amy, her face screwed into an unrecognizable mask, shoved her mother.

Lucinda's eyes widened, and she tumbled.

The gun flew from her hand and landed a few steps below me.

A shoulder crashed against the bannister and a baluster broke. Time slowed as Lucinda fell past me.

I scrambled for the weapon then looked down.

At the bottom of the stairs, Lucinda's body sprawled at odd angles (legs didn't turn that way—*necks* didn't turn that way). A pool of blood spread beneath her.

"Oh no." Amy's voice was a whisper. "I didn't mean it."

"You saved me." I climbed the stairs, wrapped her in a hug, and hid her gaze in my shoulder. "It'll be okay." It wouldn't. "We'll call for help."

Chapter Eighteen

I held tight to the shaking child in my arms. "It's okay." It wasn't. I stroked Amy's hair. "It's okay."

Amy shook harder.

"Amy." I softened my voice to a whisper. "We need to call for help."

Her arms tightened around me.

"Maybe Bernie's back from the market." I wasn't that lucky. "I'm going to yell for her."

Amy's chin bobbed against my shoulder.

"Bernie!" More of a bellow than a yell.

Bernie did not appear.

Drat.

"Sweetie, where can I find a telephone?"

"Mommy and Daddy's room."

"Will you show me?"

With her hand gripping mine hard enough to bruise my bones, Amy led me in the opposite direction of her room, opened a door, and pointed. "By the bed."

Together we approached the phone. I sat on the mattress,

pulled her into my lap, and dialed. "Would you please connect me with the police?"

"In what regard?"

"There's been an accident." In my lap, Amy stiffened. "We also need an ambulance."

The operator connected me, and I lied a second time. "There's been a terrible accident. We need help." I gave them the address and hung up.

On my lap, Amy shook hard enough to rattle her teeth.

I held her close and rubbed small circles on her back. "Do you know your daddy's phone number at work?"

"He'll think I'm a bad girl." The pain in her voice nearly broke my heart.

"No, honey. It's a mommy and daddy's job to protect their children. He'll understand. He'll protect you." Or he'd answer to me.

She thought for long seconds, then gave me the number.

"Mr. Sandhurst's office." The voice was professional. And young.

"This is Ellison Russell calling. I'm a friend of the family, and there's an emergency—"

"Amy? I'll connect you."

Seconds later Bill's voice boomed through the receiver. "Ellison? What's wrong? What's happened to Amy?"

"Amy's fine, but Lucinda fell. You need to come home. Right away."

"Fell?"

"Down the stairs."

"I'm on my way."

I carried Amy to her room and settled her in her pillows with Oliver. "Amy, did your mommy tell you to keep the medicine a secret?"

She nodded.

I took her hand in mine. "You're a good secret keeper."

She blinked.

"What happened on the stairs is our secret. We'll tell your daddy, but no one else." The poor kid had been through so much. She didn't need to be dragged through an investigation, didn't need people knowing she'd killed her mother.

"But I pushed her."

"And if you and your daddy want to tell people, you can. When the police get here, I'm telling them she fell."

Now, she frowned.

"Do you trust me?"

She nodded. Slowly.

"Where does your mommy keep her gun?" I'd left the .22 on the bedside table.

"The top drawer in the tall dresser in her bedroom."

"I should put it away. I'll be right back."

Her hand squeezed mine.

"I promise. I'll be back. We'll get through this together."

She loosened her hold on my fingers.

I returned the gun to its hiding place, then stopped at the top of the stairs. Lucinda hadn't moved, but the pool of blood was now a lake.

Ding, dong.

"Amy," I called. "The police are here. I'm going to let them in."

I descended the stairs, skirted Lucinda's body, and opened the front door.

The uniformed police officer looked over my shoulder and his eyes widened.

I stepped out of the doorway.

The police and paramedics took over. They checked for a pulse (miraculously, she had one) and moved her to a gurney.

They were loading her into the ambulance when Bill arrived. "What happened?" he demanded.

I glanced at the police officers. "She tripped and fell."

"Those damned shoes. I warned her. If I had a nickel for every time she tripped, I'd be a rich man."

He was a rich man.

"Where's Amy?"

"In her room."

"Do you need a ride to the hospital, sir?"

Bill's expression was blank. He was in shock. And the worst shocks were yet to come.

"His daughter—she's eight—is here. Upstairs in her room. She saw her mother fall and she needs her father. I'll make sure he gets to the hospital."

The officer nodded. "We have questions."

Of course he did. "Detective Jones knows where to find me."

"The homicide detective?"

"Yes."

Understanding dawned. "You're his—"

"Yes."

He nodded and left me with Bill.

"I should check on Amy." Bill moved toward the stairs.

I stopped him with a hand on his arm. "We need to talk first." We sat on the couch in the living room, and I told him everything. The apitoxin. His daughter's illness. Monica's murder. And how Amy saved me.

"She pushed her mother? You said she fell." His head fell to his hands. "What did you tell the police?"

"I told them Lucinda fell. An accident. Amy has enough to deal with."

Bill crumpled. His shoulders sagged. Twenty years snuck onto his face. His skin turned ashen. "I should have known."

I didn't argue. "You can't let Amy feel responsible for this—for any of this. She'll need counseling."

He didn't react.

"Bill!"

He looked up from the study of his hands.

"Promise me."

"I promise."

Ding, dong.

"I'll get that. You check on Amy. She needs her daddy."

The foyer still looked like a scene from a horror movie. I tiptoed around the blood and opened the door.

Anarchy frowned when he saw me. "What are you doing here?" Then he spotted the blood. "What happened?"

I swallowed. "Lucinda had a fall."

AT EXACTLY SIX O'CLOCK, Anarchy arrived.

My stomach flipped when I saw him. I'd lied to him. And we couldn't start our lives together with that lie between us. The other secrets I kept? They lived in the past. As far as I was concerned, they could stay there. But Amy? That was fresh and new. I offered him a tremulous smile.

"You look gorgeous."

"You, too," I murmured.

Behind me, Grace giggled (she'd skipped working on her oral history project to help me get ready). She could giggle all she wanted—I was right. In his charcoal suit paired with a red tie, gorgeous wasn't a strong enough word.

"Where are you going?" Grace asked.

"Nabil's," he replied.

My favorite restaurant.

We didn't talk on the drive to the Plaza. Nerves stilled my tongue.

I could do this. I had to do this.

We followed the maître d' to an intimate table in the restaurant's far corner.

Candlelight flickered. Soft music played.

Anarchy reached across the table and took my hand.

"Wait." A sinking feeling—my life was about to implode —choked me.

"What's wrong?" Concern wrinkled his brow.

"There's something you should know."

He waited for more.

"Lucinda Sandhurst didn't fall."

His brows rose. "What happened?"

"She was holding me at gunpoint—"

"Gunpoint?" His voice was gunshot loud. The other diners turned and stared at us.

I couldn't lie to him. "Amy pushed her."

He let go of my hand, and my heart cringed.

"Lucinda died on her way to the hospital." Her death was a homicide. Amy was responsible. And Anarchy followed the rules. It was what he did, who he was. "Tell me everything."

I took a deep breath and began. "You remember the apitoxin I found in Amy's medicine cabinet?"

He nodded.

"Lucinda was dosing Amy with it."

His face was a grim mask. "Why?"

"To make her sick."

His eyes narrowed.

"She wanted Bill to pay attention to her. Amy would get sick, Lucinda would save her, and Bill would call her an angel." That was tricky. What came next was worse. "She also used the apitoxin to murder Monica."

"How?"

"She scratched her with something dipped in the venom and stole her allergy kit."

"Why did Monica say she was my wife?" Anarchy's voice was flat.

"I don't know." The one person who could tell us was dead. Nor could she tell us if she'd been having an affair. "Maybe to make sure I'd see her. Maybe she wanted to enlist our help without getting too involved."

Anarchy tapped his fist against his chin. His eyes were as hard as I'd ever seen them. "You told the police Lucinda's fall was an accident." He rubbed his palm across his forehead. "You lied."

This was it. This was the end. My throat swelled, and I took a sip of water. "That little girl has been through hell."

"It's not your call, Ellison."

"Her mother poisoned her to manipulate her father. Then this happened. If I'd told the truth, everyone would know she'd killed her mother. She has enough to handle."

"What about Monica Alexander?"

I knew what he'd say next.

"She deserves justice." There. He'd said it.

My mouth was desert dry. I forced a small sip of water. "She adored children. She spent her life making sure they had healthy childhoods. I'd bet she'd want us to keep quiet about her murder. Especially when speaking up could mean ruining Amy's life." I swallowed hard. "It's not as if Lucinda can be punished for her crimes."

"Does Bill Sandhurst know?"

"I told him this afternoon. About Amy."

Anarchy raked his fingers through his hair. "Why did you go to the Sandhursts' by yourself?"

"I worried Amy was in danger. I called the precinct before

I went. I left a message telling you where I'd be. I asked you to come."

His frown was fearsome. "I didn't get the message."

"Then why were you there?"

"While the judge considered the warrant for the apothecary's records, I visited the last auto-body repair shop. Lucinda's Volvo had significant damage to the front right fender." He stared at me. "She tried to kill you."

"Twice. The first time...maybe she thought Monica left me a message. I don't know. The second time, she'd admitted poisoning her child. Amy saved me." I twisted the napkin in my lap. "I left the decision to come clean with Bill. He'll speak with a counselor about what's best for Amy. Maybe they'll decide to admit the truth. Maybe they won't."

"That's not how this works." He crossed his arms over his chest.

"I told you because I didn't want this secret between us." And now I'd lost him. "The law wouldn't find Amy guilty of anything. She defended me. I lied to keep her out of the spotlight."

The waiter arrived at our table with a bottle of Dom Perignon and two Champagne flutes. He didn't know Anarchy had changed his mind.

I dropped my hands to my lap and hid their shaking.

Before Anarchy could send him away, the waiter popped the cork and poured wine into the glasses. Then he settled the bottle into an ice bucket and backed away.

"Looks like you had something special planned." Sadness twisted my insides.

Anarchy's arms remained firmly crossed. "I did."

"I'm sorry." My jaw ached with unshed tears, and I stared at him, memorizing the color of his hair, the small scar on his right hand, the curve of his neck. "I'm sorry I did this to us. But

I'd do it again. I didn't follow the rules, but I did the right thing."

"Ellison..." His voice was raw.

I closed my eyes, closed out the next moment. This was going to hurt a thousand times worse than Henry's death. "You don't have to take me home. I'll call a cab."

He didn't respond.

Tears leaked past my lashes, but I kept my eyes firmly shut. I wasn't ready to see the end written across his face.

"Ellison." That raw, pained voice again. I'd hurt him. Badly.

I covered my mouth to hold in a sob.

"Ellison. Look at me."

I owed him that. I opened my eyes.

Anarchy knelt in front of me. Knelt and held a ring box.

"What are you doing?"

"Asking you to marry me."

"But..."

"We won't always agree, but as long as we're honest with each other, I like our chances. And I love you. More than I can possibly express. Please, make me the happiest man on earth. Say you'll be my wife."

The sob I'd been holding in ripped from my throat.

He opened the ring box, and I gasped. Jinx had been wrong. Not three karats. The diamond in the box was at least four.

"This was my grandmother's, but if you don't like it..."

"I love it. I love you. Yes."

"Yes?"

Tears ran down my cheeks. "Yes."

He slipped the ring on my finger, and the people around us clapped.

Then he stood, pulled me to my feet, and kissed me.

The restaurant faded away. We were the only two people in the world. He wiped away my tears with the pad of his thumb. "Now what?"

"Champagne?"

We sat, and he lifted his glass. "To the most beautiful, talented, caring woman I know."

"To the best man I've ever met."

We touched the flutes' rims and sipped.

"When would you like to get married?" he asked.

I thought about Mother, and the arguments waiting for me. I thought about engagement parties. I thought about the circus and all the monkeys in my future—all I wanted from my future was Anarchy. "Can we elope?"

Also by Julie Mulhern

The Country Club Murders

The Deep End

Guaranteed to Bleed

Clouds in My Coffee

Send in the Clowns

Watching the Detectives

Cold as Ice

Shadow Dancing

Back Stabbers

Telephone Line

Stayin' Alive

Killer Queen

Night Moves

The Poppy Fields Adventures

Fields' Guide to Abduction

Fields' Guide to Assassins

Fields' Guide to Voodoo

Fields' Guide to Fog

Fields' Guide to Pharaohs

Fields' Guide to Dirty Money